G R JORDAN

The Wrong Man

A Highlands and Islands Detective Thriller #41

The cover-up, more than the initial wrongdoing, is what is most likely to bring you down.

MADELINE ALBRIGHT

Contents

Foreword

The events of this book, while based around real and also fictitious locations around Scotland, are entirely fictional and all characters do not represent any living or deceased person. All companies are fictitious representations. This novel is best read while painting small miniature figures whilst wearing a dice t-shirt.

Acknowledgments

To Ken, Jean, Colin, Evelyn, John and Rosemary for your work in bringing this novel to completion, your time and effort is deeply appreciated.

Books by G R Jordan

The Highlands and Islands Detective series (Crime)

1. Water's Edge
2. The Bothy
3. The Horror Weekend
4. The Small Ferry
5. Dead at Third Man
6. The Pirate Club
7. A Personal Agenda
8. A Just Punishment
9. The Numerous Deaths of Santa Claus
10. Our Gated Community
11. The Satchel
12. Culhwch Alpha
13. Fair Market Value
14. The Coach Bomber
15. The Culling at Singing Sands
16. Where Justice Fails
17. The Cortado Club
18. Cleared to Die
19. Man Overboard!
20. Antisocial Behaviour
21. Rogues' Gallery
22. The Death of Macleod - Inferno Book 1

Kirsten Stewart Thrillers (Thriller)

1. A Shot at Democracy
2. The Hunted Child
3. The Express Wishes of Mr MacIver
4. The Nationalist Express
5. The Hunt for 'Red Anna'
6. The Execution of Celebrity
7. The Man Everyone Wanted
8. Busman's Holiday
9. A Personal Favour
10. Infiltrator
11. Implosion
12. Traitor

Jac Moonshine Thrillers

1. Jac's Revenge
2. Jac for the People
3. Jac the Pariah

Siobhan Duffy Mysteries

1. A Giant Killing
2. Death of the Witch
3. The Bloodied Hands
4. A Hermit's Death

The Contessa Munroe Mysteries (Cozy Mystery)

1. Corpse Reviver
2. Frostbite
3. Cobra's Fang

The Patrick Smythe Series (Crime)

1. The Disappearance of Russell Hadleigh
2. The Graves of Calgary Bay
3. The Fairy Pools Gathering

Austerley & Kirkgordon Series (Fantasy)

1. Crescendo!
2. The Darkness at Dillingham
3. Dagon's Revenge
4. Ship of Doom

Supernatural and Elder Threat Assessment Agency (SETAA) Series (Fantasy)

1. Scarlett O'Meara: Beastmaster

Island Adventures Series (Cosy Fantasy Adventure)

1. Surface Tensions

Dark Wen Series (Horror Fantasy)

Chapter 01

Emmett Grump pulled up to the Inverness Police Station, parking the car in the snow-covered area behind the station. It used to have painted lines and order to it but now cars were possibly abandoned as his driving instructor would have put it. Anything over two feet from the curb was abandoned, not parked.

They kept saying winter would be gone soon, but it hadn't, lingering on as ever. Did it linger, though? This was February, wasn't it? No, it had turned into March, and Emmett had barely noticed.

He'd been so busy tidying up the flat in Glasgow. He'd been getting ready to move up and, what with assisting Sabine as well, the time had flown.

Sabine Ferguson was to be his sergeant in what would be a reversal of roles. Emmett had worked for the Arts team in Glasgow under Clarissa Urquhart, but now he was moving up to his own team. A cold case division, it had been described as, and DCI Macleod had said Emmett would be perfect for it.

Emmett wasn't sure why, but the opportunity to progress, to become a detective inspector, had been too much to resist. He was only an acting DI at the moment, but hopefully in the not-too-far future, he would be promoted properly. In the meantime, he would run the division along with Sabine. It was small, but Macleod had said that it could grow in the future, depending on how Emmett did.

Emmett was happy with that, a chance to take something and run with it. Sabine had been excited as well. Emmett had grown to be rather fond of her, and the pair of them saw a lot of each other outside of work. There was nothing amorous in it. They were just good friends. He had got her into role-playing games and board games. It had helped her become a geek like him. He was a geek, and he knew it. At his age, lots of other adults saw playing games as far beneath them, but not Emmett.

He enjoyed the role-play, enjoyed the fantasy of being a warrior in a far-off plane, being a space marine. Emmett loved painting the tiny figures for the game. The box containing his works in progress had been the first to come up, packed away in the car, with his paints and brushes. He was going to be careful, though. He didn't want to flood the office too quickly with things like that.

Emmett had asked Macleod about a dress code, and should he be like Macleod in wearing a shirt and tie? But Macleod had pointed to Hope, and then Clarissa. Well, Emmett had thought, Hope had that figure. She could wear almost anything and look good in it. And as for Clarissa, he wasn't following her dress sense. Tartan everywhere.

Emmett had gone back to Macleod, and Macleod told him to wear whatever he wanted. Macleod didn't care about that. He cared more about how Emmett got on with the cases.

So, Emmett now emerged from the car, dressed in his blue jeans, a t-shirt under a jumper which had an enormous dragon on the front. Being cold, however, he took his coat, a bomber jacket, out of the rear of the car, zipped it up, and opened the boot.

He was able to take two boxes before closing it, and marched through the rear doors of the station, up the stairs, and down to the far end of a lonely corridor.

Macleod had been very apologetic about this. His room was almost a broom cupboard. There was space at one end for a desk, for Emmett. A small desk was included for Sabine, and there wasn't much room in between.

Emmett had got a couple of pegs fixed onto the wall so they could hang coats. There was a filing cabinet, a tall wardrobe that had clearly been a rescue case, possibly from a skip. A radiator covered another part of the wall, taking up space.

He dropped the boxes onto his desk, took off his coat, and hung it up. There was a small window from which he could see a part of Inverness he didn't recognise.

There were residential houses displaying their backs to the station. It certainly wasn't as good as the view Macleod had up in his office, and the DCI complained about that.

Emmett wasn't sure how he felt about Macleod. He'd known the name, of course. Everyone knew the name. DCI Seoras Macleod. 'Grumpy.' Emmett had been called 'Grumpy' when he started, but due to his surname.

Grump wasn't the most dynamic family tag, was it? And Emmett had struggled to fit into teams. But he'd been useful. And that was the trick. Always be useful, see what they couldn't. Always find out what they can't. And be prepared to help your colleagues.

His last post on the Arts team had been strange. Clarissa Urquhart, for example. He'd never had a boss like her. And at

Christmas, he'd watched her chase after a carriage, put her life on the line to save what was effectively an overblown piece of wood. An expensive one, yes, but there wasn't a person attached to it. *What madness*, he'd thought. And he told her so.

In fairness, she'd taken the rebuke.

Emmett unpacked one of his boxes in the far corner of his desk, placing several miniature figures that had an undercoat on them, ready for detailed painting. A neat wooden box held his brushes, and he took out a cup bearing a small, impish dungeon master logo on the side.

For years, he'd used that cup for his water. The paintbrushes had almost worn a groove on the side where they sat. He'd have to get some water in it soon. He took the other box and removed some of his gear; it was the police work box, the stuff he had to bring with him from the other office.

Emmett pulled open several of the desk drawers, and then he spied an envelope. It was on Sabine's desk, not his. He walked over and picked it up. It was brown, plain, but felt quite chunky.

The name on the front simply read, 'Acting DI Grump.' He pulled out the contents. Inside was a list of cold cases and there were plenty. That was the thing about police work. People thought everything got solved; everything wound up in the end. But here was a list stretching back thirty-plus years.

Well, he wouldn't be getting all of those done. He'd have to prioritise, work out what was best to do. At the bottom, it said that the files for most cases were located, or at least copies of, in his filing cabinet. They must have been old because the modern cases were all on the system.

Emmett pulled open the drawers and sighed when he looked at the contents. They'd just been stuck in. They weren't categorised. There was no logic to where everything was. He glanced at the tabs on the files to see the different case numbers, the years they were from.

There was a knock at the door.

'Come in,' said Emmett, not looking up.

'I hope you're getting on well. You're prompt anyway.'

Emmett looked up to see DCI Macleod standing in the doorway. He'd clearly just arrived, his long coat still on, as well as the fedora hat.

'We'll have the place ship-shape in no time,' said Emmett. 'Just awaiting Sabine.'

'Were you not stopping at the same hotel?'

'No, no,' said Emmett. 'I've got some digs. And besides, I was in Glasgow this morning. Just brought a few things up.'

'Glasgow this morning?' said Macleod, his face frowning. 'What time did you leave?'

'Oh, it wasn't long. About half five, six.'

Macleod shrugged his shoulders. 'Don't overdo it,' he said. 'You need to bed in. Let people know you're here.'

'Are you saying they'll miss me?'

'Well,' said Macleod, 'I'm sorry you're stuck at the far end here. You're kind of out of the way, but when you work a cold case, maybe it's best to be out of sight. Things get stirred up. People don't like issues coming back that they think are over and done.'

'I was planning on looking through the cases,' said Emmett. 'I'll try to dig out what's reasonable to have a look at, what we can best have a go at. Then I'll bring them up to you. Just to make sure you approve of where I'm heading.'

Macleod strode over and put his hand on the file that was at the very front of the cabinet drawer Emmett had opened.

5

Macleod pulled it out and dropped it on Sabine's desk.

'That's Sabine's,' said Emmett. 'I'm the one here. You can tell because it's got—'

'It's got the little men. He paints the little men.' Macleod laughed. 'Clarissa went on and on to me about your little men. Why do you paint little men? She doesn't see it as art.'

'Well, I do,' said Emmett rather dryly.

'Don't ask me,' said Macleod. 'I know nothing about either. But what I do know is you're going to be investigating this case first.'

Emmett shut the drawer and sat down in his seat behind his desk. He flipped open the file.

'Well, the case of DC Gavin Isbister,' said Emmett.

'Orca.'

'Orca?' said Emmett. 'Was he big?'

'Not the whale. Orcadian. But he was a chunky man as well. Good detective, thorough, sincere, not turned easily.'

Emmett was scanning the documents in front of him.

'Good detective?' he said to Macleod. 'Talks about corruption here with regards to some arrest. Possible murderer?'

Macleod took a deep breath. 'Gavin Isbister was no murderer. I'm convinced of that.'

'So you've looked at this as well?'

'Isbister was my colleague for a short time.'

'How short a time?' asked Emmett.

'He was my colleague at the time he died. I had been taken away when his death happened. Or at least, what they believe was his death. They think he committed suicide. Ran away. No body ever found.'

Macleod turned and looked out the window. He drew another deep breath.

'Your view's even worse than mine. Hope's got the best view. Do you know that, Emmett? I miss that office. It was good. But I wouldn't be here, and you wouldn't be here, if I hadn't stepped up. I've got to make opportunities for everyone else now. I've got to do some good police work.' For a moment, Macleod seemed to drift away.

'You've got to do some good police work, Emmett. This is the case to start with. Don't look at anything else yet. Straight into this. Do it quietly; do it efficiently.'

'It's obviously personal to you,' said Emmett. 'Didn't you look into it at the time?'

'Of course I looked into it,' said Macleod, almost testily. 'No evidence to the contrary. When you read it, you'll find out. Couldn't prove anything. Had to just get on. It's never sat with me.'

'Well, why don't you join me on it?'

'I'm too close,' said Macleod. 'Needs a fresh pair of eyes.'

'And you've been waiting this long.'

Emmett wanted to say, 'I don't believe you.' But as this was his first day in a new job, and the man who had helped him get that position was the one he was about to say he didn't believe, he thought better of it.

Truthfully, he wished Sabine would come in. Emmett wasn't good in one-to-one conversations. He preferred to drop back, preferred to listen and observe, watch what was going on. In that way, Sabine was a great foil for him. Working under Clarissa, Sabine had taken the lead, and Emmett had picked out what was wrong, worked in the background. He wasn't sure how it was going to operate now. At least it was his friend he was working with.

'Just find out for me; get to the truth,' said Macleod. 'I want

7

nothing else. I don't want to be sheltered if you find something about Isbister. Just get to the truth. It's what we do. It's why we are here, okay?'

'Always,' said Emmett.

Macleod reached over with his hand, and Emmett stood up from his chair to shake it.

'Welcome to the new job. Welcome to me and working directly with me. You don't go through anyone else. Don't let anyone borrow you. Your job is the cold case. My door is always open upstairs. I have a secretary who'll tell you I'm busy or this or that. But if you really need me, the door's open. Only knock! Clarissa just barges in.'

Emmett had to fight back a laugh. 'I think you'll find I'm different from DI Urquhart.'

'One can only pray,' said Macleod. He turned away and then he halted. 'Oh, while I'm here. A little welcome present.' From his pocket, Macleod pulled out a tiny figure inside a plastic case. Emmett took it from him and almost laughed.

The figure had long tentacles coming from it and was ugly in the extreme. Multiple mouths with sharp teeth. Emmett wondered about the colours the creature should sport. Then he looked up at Macleod.

'I know you're a detective, but how did you know this one? I don't have it,' he said.

'I asked Sabine. I have no idea what that even is.'

'What it is, is appreciated. Thank you.'

'And remember, it's Seoras,' said Macleod as he left. 'But not how Clarissa says it. She says it with contempt. Just Seoras. Maybe how Hope says it.'

'Yes, Seoras.'

Macleod left the office and walked down the long corridor

8

to the stairs. On the top floor, he strode to his office, where he opened the door and shut it quickly behind him. From inside his jacket, he removed an envelope before taking out a small piece of paper from inside. There, in capitals and blue ink, was the legend: 'POOR ISBISTER. HOW DID YOU FINISH HIM?'

Chapter 02

Sabine Ferguson stepped out of her car and kicked the tyres. A flat. A flat on her first day in her new job. She had texted Emmett to tell him, and it had taken her a while to change it over.

Emmett had told her to get the tyre changed properly. In truth, what was happening that morning? It wasn't like they were in the middle of a case. However, there had been something in his voice. Sabine Ferguson had known Emmett now for a while and was extremely fond of the man. He was unlike most other men around her.

Sabine labelled men into three categories. There were the jerks, the ones that looked at you, who just wanted you for your figure. They wanted to use you for their own pleasure, their delight. They wanted you to look how they wanted you to look. She was tall; she was in good shape, and Sabine thought she had a decent smile.

Maybe it was all these things that attracted the wrong type. Anyway, she learnt long ago how to deal with them and get rid of them. And then there were the other types: Ross, Macleod, Perry. Just ordinary, decent guys. They treated you with respect. They worked with you. You had a laugh with them.

Yes, normal people.

Then there was the other type. The ones you fell for. The ones who wanted to build you up, wanted to hold you, wanted to be with you, could keep you warm. And you wanted them in a big way. It had been a while since any of those sorts of guys. Not that she was looking for one. And then there was Emmett.

What was Emmett? He was like the second sort. She had fun with him. They went and played his role play and board games. But he was also like the third sort in that he was interested in her and what she did—he'd even gone to look at artwork that he had no idea about. They'd been to cinemas together. He was like a best friend, and yet they hadn't known each other that long.

She was annoyed as well with him, though. He'd found digs, and she hadn't. Maybe he just wasn't as picky as she was because she wanted a flat with a view. Emmett had found a small house on the outskirts of Inverness.

He was renting it. It had a garden, even though she'd never known him to be a gardener. Although nothing too big, he said it had a room where the sun shone in and he could sit and paint his models. It also had a fantastic dining room, and he was going to get a table designed for board games. He might get eight to ten players around it. He needed to get into a gaming group. Sabine needed to join, too.

Sabine wrapped her fleece up round her, grabbed her bag from the back of the car along with a box, and strode into the Inverness police station. She had hiking boots on today, but the snow was thick and she felt the chill as she approached.

She saw DC Perry coming the other way, a detective working within Hope's team.

11

'Miss Ferguson,' said Perry. He almost bowed to her as she walked past. 'Welcome to the madhouse,' he said.

'Where are you off to?' asked Sabine, looking bemusedly at him. Perry was wearing a shirt under a suit jacket and was walking over to where the smokers would gather. There were none there at the moment.

'Just off for my virtual fag,' he said. 'You can quit the sticks, but you can't quit the feeling of being out here. And all that fresh air.'

Sabine shook her head. Perry was a strange one. She climbed up the stairs, turned down a corridor, and walked past all the nameplates of other groups and departments. She then found the rather less-walked corridor and strode to the end. 'Cold Case Unit,' it said on the door. It didn't even have Emmett's name yet.

He was going to be an acting DI, but this was so Emmett. The man didn't care what anybody else thought. He didn't care about prestige. All Emmett would care about was getting on with the case and then getting back to his figures or to his friends. She kicked the door with her feet, her hands full, and it swung open. She stepped inside and dumped her box down on her desk.

Somehow, in such a tight space, Emmett was standing between the desks, writing on a whiteboard that was attached to the wall. It hadn't been there previously.

'Morning; sorry about that,' she said. 'What on earth?'

'Close the door—take your jacket off,' said Emmett. 'We've got work.'

'What? What do you mean we've got work? You said to get the wheel done.'

'Yes, it's fine, but we've got work. Look,' said Emmett.

'Just a moment,' said Sabine. She unzipped her fleece, looked around, and hung it up on the other hook beside Emmett's coat. 'Do I not get a coffee first?'

'Oh, I haven't had time for one,' said Emmett. 'I had to pop out and buy this.' Sabine looked up at the whiteboard. 'We need it. There's not a lot of room in here, so I thought it would go there. Look. This is the case.'

He pointed to a picture. The man on it was chunky with tattoos on his forearms. He had a beard, albeit light brown, and shortish brown hair that was tussled.

'Who's that?' asked Sabine.

'That's DC Gavin Isbister, also known as Orca. Orcadian man. That's from Orkney.'

'Oh, duh,' said Sabine.

'He's a former colleague of DCI Macleod.'

'Right, what is he to us?' asked Sabine.

'He's at the heart of our first cold case. Macleod's been down here and told us this is what we're doing.'

'Whoa,' said Sabine. 'So our first case is digging up something on Macleod's old mate, really?'

'I know,' said Emmett. 'Park that thought for a minute. DC Isbister and DC Macleod, as he was back then, were called to the body of a Glaswegian man, Ian McCollum, up in Pitlochry. He was murdered. Now, Ian McCollum was a gangster belonging to Stu McIntosh's gang.'

'Stu McIntosh? You're kidding. He was a nutter.'

'He was a nutter. A nutter that was difficult to bring down. They got him, though. Well, put it this way: he was taken out of the picture. Anyway, in this case, you had the deceased Ian McCollum, one of McIntosh's men. The investigation into it brought up Simon Matthews as a suspect, a local man. It was a little strange, though. Simon Matthews was someone who was looking into gangs. A sort of early-day Roger Cook.'

'So what, they think Matthews killed McCollum?'

'Well, the official report says that Simon Matthews was found dead several days later. A murder weapon was on him. However, the fingerprints of Isbister were found on the weapon. When that was discovered, Isbister vanished from Pitlochry. He disappeared, leaving only a suicide note.'

'What?' asked Sabine.

'Exactly,' said Emmett. 'Case was closed because Isbister never turned up, so they concluded he must have killed Simon Matthews and done a runner.'

'But why kill Simon Matthews?'

'The official reports say that Matthews and Isbister got together to kill Ian McCollum. McCollum, being part of Stu McIntosh's gang, was someone that Simon Matthews wanted to highlight. I'm not sure why particularly. McCollum's report says nothing about that.'

'So where was Macleod then when his mate turned around and killed somebody and legged it, leaving a suicide note?' asked Sabine.

'He'd been taken off the case and sent back to Glasgow to a different case, for some reason. It's not clear here.'

'Well, why don't we go up and ask him?'

'No,' said Emmett.

'Why not?'

'Because he's put us onto this. Macleod specifically asked, above all the other cases in that file, to look into this. This is not a cold case file. This is an occurrence that's signed, sealed, and delivered. He's committed suicide. We haven't found the body. He's leapt into the sea. He's done something like that.'

'He's not going to leap into the sea in Pitlochry, is he?' blurted Sabine.

'Into a loch, whatever,' said Emmett. He stopped, looking up at the board in front of him. 'Something isn't right.'

'What's not right is the fact I haven't had a coffee yet, and you're dumping all this on me already.'

'No, no,' said Emmett. 'Something's not right. The entire way this has come up, how it's being brought to us. I'm not happy with it.'

'Well, get up those stairs and tell him.'

'No, that's the last thing we need to do. He's brought this for a reason, Macleod, but he's not telling me. He said he wants a fresh set of eyes on it. That's why he's not investigating it.'

'Well, that could be true.'

'Really?' said Emmett. 'It's Macleod. Why wouldn't he investigate it himself? Who would he trust? Especially if it's bugged him for this length of time. But also, there's no way he would have left it this length of time. This is twenty-five, thirty years ago. The people in this, some of them, will be old. Older than him. He wouldn't wait.'

'If you talk to Hope, he's changed a lot over the last lot of years. He might not have been in a position mentally to—'

'No, he'd have been in a worse position. He'd have been absolutely driven with his work. Not with everything else,' said Emmett. He sat down in his seat at the desk.

'So, what do we do first?' asked Sabine.

'We find out about Isbister. Does he have family? Did he have a wife at the time? Where is the wife? Enough for us to get started on.'

'Well, I'm going to unpack,' said Sabine.

'I wouldn't unpack too much. We're going to head off and

15

find her. Could be a day's travel away,' said Emmett.

'Well, I need to get this stuff out of a box,' said Sabine. She started to unpack, opening her desk drawers, putting away her work gear. There was still more in Glasgow to come up, but she'd get that as and when. She stopped for a moment and looked over.

Emmett was sitting behind his desk and picked up one figure, twirling it over in front of his eyes. He was working out how to paint it, and yet he wasn't. The man was thinking—this was how he worked. He would almost disappear within himself.

'Shall I get coffee?' asked Sabine.

'You're still unpacking, I can do that. I think we have to use the kitchen round here.'

'There's no kitchen here. It'll be on the next floor. We're not doing that,' said Sabine. Emmett shrugged his shoulders. 'You need somewhere for coffee. Coffee in here okay, we need a kettle. We need to set up for us.'

'Set it up then,' said Emmett.

'Oh no,' said Sabine. 'We're not doing that. You're not going off on the case and ditching me to do this. I may be a sergeant, and you may be acting DI, and you may be on the up but I'm not getting treated like the skivvy.'

She saw Emmett suddenly look incredibly hurt. 'You're no skivvy!' he said. 'We're a team. You know that, don't you?' She looked over at him with a smile, but he still had a worried look on his face.

'What?' she said.

'Are you still annoyed?' asked Emmett. 'I took the house because we need our own space. We need two places. Some-where we can go with—'

'Of course, I'm not annoyed.'

'But you thought a flat share would be good. The same place, you—'

'It's fine,' said Sabine. It wasn't fine. She liked the idea of being around Emmett, a lot more than she'd realised at the time.

'You finish unpacking,' he said. 'I'll get a kettle from somewhere. They'll have one at Argos or somewhere like that, won't they?'

He stood up, grabbed his coat off the hook, and went to leave. But he stopped at the door and turned back to Sabine.

'When we get back from this, we'll have a look for somewhere for yourself. I'll help you look for the flat. I didn't mean it to—'

'It's fine. You're probably right,' said Sabine.

Emmett left and shut the door behind him, leaving Sabine in the room. It was quite a cold room, although the whiteboard, now with pictures on it, and the beginnings of a case was bringing it to life.

Why had Emmett renting a house bothered her so much? Why had his desire to have his own place affected her? They'd seen so much of each other recently, but they weren't anything special, were they? They were just friends. He didn't say it with any amorous intent, did he? She didn't, did she?

Sabine gave her head a shake and continued to unpack. He was going to get a kettle for her—if that wasn't friendship, she didn't know what was.

Chapter 03

Much to Emmett's surprise, Sabine found out that Isabelle, Isbister's wife, was currently living in Pitlochry. They hadn't lived there at the time of the murder, Isbister had been working out of Glasgow along with Macleod, and so the pair decided to visit her. It would also give them a chance to have a good look around Pitlochry at the various sites that had been involved in the case.

The snow was thick on the mountains, but the sun was up, and the air was cool and crisp as they drove past the Cairngorms, routing out the other side on cleared roads. Sabine watched her colleague as he sat in the passenger seat.

He had the case file with him, leafing through it repeatedly. The car was playing heavy metal music, something that Sabine found refreshing. It wasn't quite her—she was more of a rock chick, as they put it. This music was maybe slightly too loud for her, too intense. But Emmett loved it. It was bizarre how, with all the noise going on, he sat there concentrating, working away on the document. He had a pen out, highlighting different bits and pieces. She queried this at one point, until he pointed out that these were photocopies, not the original.

They turned off at Pitlochry. The road gave no hint of

the town that lay beyond, and wound through trees on the outskirts before pulling into the rather quaint town centre.

The house they were looking for was on the other side of Pitlochry, slightly removed from the town. It took another ten minutes to find it once they were clear of the town centre. It was on the slope of a hill, a perfect lawn obscured in white. There were trees on either side, making the property hard to see into. Sabine drove the car up a pristine, snow-laden driveway along which cars hadn't been since the last fall.

When Sabine parked the car, she could see a face at the window. It was a man, maybe in his sixties. She stepped out, feeling the cold almost immediately, and took her fleece from the rear seat, zipping it up tight and planting her hands into the pockets. Emmett stepped out of the other side of the car, ignoring his jacket and making a beeline for the front door. The dragon on his jumper shone as the light bounced off it.

Sabine always wondered if this was the right look, now that Emmett was going to be leading a department. She loved him like that. She really did. It was him. He didn't care about how he dressed. Emmett loved his logos. He liked his sloppy jeans. Never would he judge anybody else by their dress. He rarely made a comment about how she was dressed, but he liked her best in her t-shirt and jeans. She could tell from the look on his face.

Together, they approached the front door and rapped a large knocker. They could hear movement behind the red door and as it was pulled open, they saw a woman in the later years of her life. It was strange, for the picture they had of Gavin Isbister had him in his forties.

The woman's face was taut, and she wore black glasses, large and round, but her eyes were sunken behind them. Her hair was wild, crinkly white, but also had not been brushed. It barely reached her neck, but it was long enough on top to look like it had been transplanted from a mad professor. She wore a grey cardigan with a black top underneath. Her hands were wrinkled, as well as her neck, which showed several veins.

'Hello?' said the woman.

'Hi. My name's Acting DI Emmett Grump; this is DS Ferguson. We're from Inverness.'

'And?'

'I'd like to talk to you about your husband,' said Emmett.

'My husband? He's inside if you wish to—'

'No, no,' said Emmett. 'Your first husband, Gavin.'

'Why? Gavin's in the past,' she said. 'Why do you want to come here and talk about him? You don't need to talk about Gavin. Gavin's dead, Gavin's long dead.'

'I appreciate it's difficult,' said Sabine. 'But we need to look into this. We've been tasked—'

'Tasked?' the woman interrupted. 'Who tasked you?'

'We're a cold case unit,' said Emmett. 'It's our job. We want to review what went on and see if there's anything we can bring to the case. On that basis, I'd like to speak to you.'

Sabine wanted to step inside out of the cold, to be invited through, but the woman wasn't having it. She could see that Emmett was feeling the cold more, and she was thankful she had her fleece on.

'Can you tell me about your husband?' asked Emmett.

'Gavin was unstable,' said the woman. 'Always unstable, and off to solve it on his own, along with that Matthews man. I don't know how they fell out, I don't know why he killed him. At least he did the best thing, went and topped himself.'

'Do you really see it like that?' asked Sabine.

'Definitely see it like that. Can you imagine the shame of him being behind bars? Besides, he was a copper. They'd go for him in there, wouldn't they? Yes, he just chickened out. He just left it. It's hard enough to bring—well, I was fortunate to marry again.'

'And you came here,' said Emmett. 'Why are you living in Pitlochry? Doesn't it bring back memories?'

'I wasn't here,' said the woman. 'I wasn't the one who killed anyone here. Why shouldn't I be here? It's a lovely place. Besides, my second husband—he likes it here.'

'Had Gavin ever been depressed in his work before the suicide note? Had he ever gone to a point of seeking to end it?' asked Sabine.

'He was always unstable. I keep telling you that. What's with the questions, anyway? Why? Why do you come here and ask this?'

'What would you say if someone said that he was framed? That he didn't actually do it? That he—' asked Emmett.

'Who said he was framed? I'm telling you now, I knew Gavin. He wasn't an amiable man to live with. They're like that from up there, aren't they, though? Why the hell did I marry an Orcadian? They don't even speak properly. They don't even—'

The woman continued to rant. Sabine watched Emmett's face. He was soaking it all in. She could tell something was clicking with him. The woman was very bitter—extremely bitter for the time that had passed.

She'd moved on, thought Sabine. *He'd done the right thing by her, she had said. Gavin had killed himself. She'd come here. She was now living in the place where he'd committed a murder, and yet, she seemed happy enough with it. The house was impressive,*

21

though.

'Are you all right there, Belle?'

The voice came from behind Isabelle, and a man entered the scene. He was over six-feet, dwarfing Emmett, but going eye to eye with Sabine. As he eyed her up, she thought of him as one of those men. He wasn't attending to his wife's difficulties, but was coming to have a look. He'd glanced briefly at Emmett and then taken a long stare at Sabine.

'We're just looking to speak to your wife,' said Emmett.

Sabine looked beyond the man to the hall and noted several pictures. 'Maybe we could come inside and talk there,' said Sabine.

'No, you don't.' The man stepped out, putting his hand on Sabine's shoulder. 'I think you need to go, little lady.'

Little, thought Sabine. I'm almost as tall as him. I could take him down.

'I think you should take your hand off the sergeant,' said Emmett.

'Why? I think you should leave.'

'But we will leave, sir,' said Emmett. 'However, first, you will take your hand off the sergeant.'

'Are you threatening me?'

'No, but that looks like an assault if you keep going. And that's going to bring a world of pain to your door. Hands off the sergeant,' said Emmett.

The man dropped his hand off Sabine's shoulder. 'Get away. Go on. Don't come back. She doesn't want to talk about it.'

'Do you know anything about it?' asked Emmett.

'No, I don't. Never knew the man. Didn't want to know the man.'

Emmett nodded to Sabine, and the two returned to the car.

Sabine spun it around and drove out of the driveway. But Emmett indicated she should pull up down the road, so she pulled into a lay-by. Emmett turned to look at her.

'What do you make of that?' he asked.

'She's cold, isn't she? The guy she spent her life with.'

'Yes, but he killed someone. I can understand the moving on.'

'She hasn't moved on, though, has she?' said Sabine.

'No,' said Emmett. 'You clocked the pictures on the wall as well. Gavin Isbister. Several of them.'

'Why would she have them up,' asked Sabine, 'when she has a new husband?'

'Shall we pop back?' said Emmett.

He got out of the car, put on his coat this time, and Sabine wrapped up well with a scarf and hat. They walked back down the road, stopping just outside the tree line, and hopped over the fence of the house. Carefully, they made their way among the trees, staying out of view of the house, until they came to its side facing wall.

There was no window there, except for a high one, with no one in it or light on. Quickly they stole across, coming close to the front room and they could hear voices:

'You just tell them to go. Why are they here anyway? Have you been speaking to anyone?'

'I've told no one. All this time I have told no one. You understand that? He said move on. I've moved on.'

'Bullshit,' said the man. 'You've never moved on from him.'

'What do you care, anyway? It's not like you married me because you love me.'

'But you married me,' he said.

'Like I was given a choice.' Isabelle was weeping now, and

23

Sabine turned to look at Emmett. *Should they intervene?*

'Maybe I should just tell them,' said a wild Isabelle. 'Maybe I should.'

The detectives could hear the strike of the hand across her cheek and her tumble to the floor. Crockery was then broken. Sabine looked at Emmett, ready to go, but he shook his head. She implored him with her eyes, but he was resolute.

'You talk to no one about anything, understand?'

The voices calmed down, but Sabine crawled round the edge of the wall and looked in the window of the living room. Sitting on a sofa was Isabelle. Her glasses were off and she was crying.

The man had clearly moved elsewhere. She felt Emmett grab her hand and whisper to her, 'He's coming out the back door. We need to move.'

Quickly they stole back across the grass to the trees, hoping he didn't come round to see footprints. They made their way out, over the fence and off to the car. They drove back past the house again and from what they could see, no one had come round the side of the house. Snow was falling now and their tracks would be covered up.

On the third pass, they stopped and Emmett, with his binoculars, looked at the front of the house. Inside the living room, Sabine could see unclear figures.

'They're hugging. A little more than that. Drive on,' said Emmett.

'We should have stepped in.'

'No, we shouldn't,' said Emmett. 'They know we're onto something. We're on the outside looking in, carefully. They now know somebody's looking at the case, but we know nothing. I want them to think we're disappearing. We're doing routine things.

'But something's up here. I get why Macleod's on to this now. She has photos of her first husband all down the hall. And she tells us he did the right thing in killing himself and that he was always unstable. There's no love coming out of what she said.'

'There's love up on the wall,' said Sabine. 'How did they hug?'

'He was probably hugging her more than she was him.'

'That says a lot.'

'It truly does,' said Emmett.

Chapter 04

Emmett sat in the car as Sabine drove through Pitlochry and out the other side to the home of Anne Matthews. According to records, the wife of Simon Matthews had never left Pitlochry and was still living in the same house as she had been when her husband was alive. As they approached, they found the house situated with its back to the railway line, one of several houses with small gardens. A line of compactly built bungalows. Pulling up in the driveway, Sabine switched off the engine and waited for Emmett to make his move.

'Aren't we going? She'll be looking out the window,' said Sabine.

'Why didn't Macleod investigate?' said Emmett out loud. 'Isabelle Isbister has remarried, moved to Pitlochry. She's living with a man, married him, tells us to keep away. Almost gets heavy-handed with you.'

'I wouldn't have said heavy-handed,' said Sabine. 'He put his hand on my shoulder.'

'And he may have pushed on. He wasn't worried about the threat of violence. He was worried about the threat of people coming. More people being involved. It makes me wonder who he is.'

'I'm more wondering why she's here in Pitlochry. I mean, if my husband had committed suicide here, I wouldn't race back.'

'No, you wouldn't,' said Emmett. He gave a shake of his head, then stepped out of the car, catching Sabine by surprise, and she hurriedly followed. The small green door of the house had a doorbell to one side, and Emmett rang it.

There was a cheerful tune, and the door was then opened by a woman in a flowery summer dress, which struck Emmett as odd for the time of year. He was standing in his coat, chilled, and the woman beamed at the pair of them.

'Excuse me,' said Emmett. 'I'm—'

'A detective,' said the woman.

'Yes,' said Emmett, caught by surprise. 'Acting DI Emmett Grump. This is DS Sabine Ferguson. We've come down from Inverness. We'd like to talk to you about—'

'Simon,' said the woman. 'It's been a while since anyone's wanted to talk about Simon. Usually, they want to keep quiet about Simon.'

'Would it be possible to come in?' asked Sabine.

'Why?' asked the woman, her tone now a little more hostile.

'Because it's properly cold,' said Sabine, 'and I'd rather talk in there than talk out here on the doorstep.'

Emmett simply nodded. The woman took a hard look at both of them before stepping back from the door and inviting them in. Closing the door behind them, she pushed them on through to the kitchen, telling them to take up a pew at the table.

'Down from Inverness,' she said, as she turned to a kettle, lifting it and filling it with water. 'Don't think we've had many come down from Inverness before. He's up in Inverness now,

27

isn't he? He left.'

'He?' said Emmett.

'Macleod. He was Isbister's friend, colleague. Wasn't here, though. Didn't come back. I thought that he would have come back, but . . .'

'He's my boss,' said Emmett.

'Okay. And he sent you here?'

'I'm running a cold-case team. This is a cold case.'

'What is?' asked the woman.

'Before I say anything, can I just confirm you are Anne Matthews?'

'Yes. Simon's widow,' she said.

'We've been asked to look into the case again, specifically at the suicide of DC Isbister.'

'I don't know if he ever committed suicide,' said the woman. 'Maybe he did, maybe he didn't, but I doubt he killed Simon.'

'Why?' asked Sabine.

'Too convenient. Way too convenient.' The woman grabbed some cups, placed them in front of the kettle, and then turned. 'Tea? I've got all sorts of teas.'

'Coffee, if you've got it,' said Emmett.

'Well, I've got some coffee. I don't drink it myself.' The woman turned back, and Sabine saw Emmett's face. It was like he'd been told the strangest thing.

'You never left Pitlochry?' asked Sabine.

'I am not going nowhere,' said Anne Matthews. 'Simon died here. The truth died with him.'

'What do you mean by that?' asked Emmett.

'Simon was investigating some senior people. The cops were very heavy-handed when they came up. There was no thought behind what was going on behind it all. Knife placed with

Simon's body, fingerprints on the knife, Isbister's? I mean, he was a detective. He did what? Killed the man and then left him? A fingerprinted weapon with him? He was no idiot. Could have thrown it in a loch somewhere. Plenty of them about. Made no sense.'

'Why would Isbister want Simon dead? And why was Simon implicated in the death of Ian McCollum?' asked Sabine.

'Simon wasn't implicated in the death of McCollum. Simon was a figure who'd been around Ian McCollum. McCollum was talking to Simon. He had no love for McCollum, no love for Stu McIntosh's crew at all, but the thing was that Simon had been alerted that something was up. Some of Stu McIntosh's crew died rather abruptly—gangland, they said—but McIntosh wasn't at war with anyone. He'd got too big, he had his patch, nobody was stepping in.

'Simon reckoned the police didn't like that, or certainly certain elements of the police didn't like that. He thought there was something else on the go. McCollum was talking to him about it, and then McCollum was dead. Simon had been seen with McCollum; therefore, he was implicated. The next thing he was dead. Simon had released a little bit of information about some rumours regarding how the police had been dealing with McIntosh's people. And that got taken as Isbister was dirty. That's what they sold to everyone.

'It all got confused and difficult. And the next thing, Isbister's purported as having killed everybody, including himself. They tried to make it all fit whoever was behind it but then left the knife with his fingerprints on. That blew the story to my mind. But things moved on, except for Simon.'

The kettle boiled, and after a click of the switch, Anne Matthews picked up the kettle.

She went to pour, but then stopped.

'And Simon—forgotten. Everything Simon was into got forgotten. You see, that's what they wanted. Macleod never came back up. When they started, Macleod and Isbister went through the case, and they had their suspects. I think they might even have suspected that something was up in the Glasgow branch. Not all of it. There were elements. But there were elements outside of that even.'

'Can you elaborate on that?' asked Sabine.

'No, no,' said Anne, still holding the kettle above the cups. She put it down. 'Why would I? Here you come, creep in saying you're from Inverness. 'Oh, Macleod has sent us.' Now, Macleod would have come himself if he's still on the right side of this. Seems all very convenient that he got bumped up from Glasgow to Inverness. Why, I hear he's got a whole department. He was always clever with the cases, but you move ahead in work not with just the work you do, but with who you know, don't you?'

'That may be why he's in Inverness, out of the way,' said Emmett. Sabine cast a glance. Emmett didn't know him that well. He couldn't say that.

'It's a lot of trust to put on you two. Fresh faces showing here,' said Anne. 'And look at you—you don't look like a detective. You certainly don't look like you're from Glasgow. She does, though. There's a more classy style.'

'What?' asked Sabine.

'He looks like he's still a teenager,' said Anne Matthews. She poured the drinks, put the kettle down, and took them over to the table. She then stood at the window. As Emmett watched, tears were coming from her eyes. 'I still work away at it, you know. I'm quiet, but I still work away at it.'

'Well, tell me what you know then,' said Emmett. 'Let me work away at it.'

'No, no, he comes down here himself and talks to me. I'll know if he's on the take or not. I don't know you. You weren't involved and could just be feeding this back to him. You may even be a pawn.'

Emmett felt like a pawn. This wasn't like the cases he'd signed up to take.

'Look,' said Sabine. 'I'm not being funny, but what's the reluctance? Information after this time. What do you know people don't know? It can't be that much, can it?'

'Simon knew too much. And then the heavy-handed police came. Well, first Macleod was here, along with Isbister. Simon was in the mix, but they weren't convicting him. They weren't saying he was involved in it. Simon had no dealings with Isbister. Not on the sly. Not like he had with Ian McCollum, digging out his information from him. Finding out the rumours and the tales.'

'Are you aware that DC Isbister's wife now lives in Pitlochry?' asked Sabine.

'Very well aware.'

'Do you know her?' continued Sabine.

'I would know her to see. I would know him to see as well. Never met the woman to speak to,' said Anne.

'You find it strange,' asked Sabine, 'that she came back here after what happened to her husband?'

'She never came until she'd remarried,' said Anne. 'Never cared for that man. He always watches me though. He's seen me.'

'You have kids?' asked Emmett.

'Left home, had to let them go. Can't stay here with me.

They told me to leave. Somebody killed Simon. Somebody knows something here. I go to the grave all the time. Tell Simon I'll find his killer. But I don't have his skills. He was good at undercover. That's what he did. He'd worked for some papers before. Freelance often. Digging out a story during his freelance days. He never thought he'd find one right here. McCollum had come up to meet him over several days and then McCollum was dead.'

'So, if I'm understanding correctly,' said Emmett, 'you believe McCollum was telling him things. Things that were big enough to rock an establishment or certainly cause some people in the police to have problems.'

'That's the long and the short of it.'

'And then,' continued Emmett, 'you think somebody found out? They killed McCollum, and then when Macleod and Isbister were sent up, they were getting somewhere. You think they got split up, and all the people who could speak to the truth of the matter were taken out of the way?'

'I reckon so. But I haven't got the proof of anything. And if I did, I wouldn't be bringing it to you. I'd put it on the telly. Put it somewhere where it's aired publicly.'

'Why haven't they got rid of you?' asked Sabine. The woman froze and turned round.

'Is that what it is?' she said. 'Are you finally here for that?'

Emmett put his hands up. 'No weapons. No, nothing. I've been sent to find out the truth of the matter. And that's what I'm going to do. I'm not here to kill anyone.' Sabine looked over at Emmett, dressed in his jeans and jumper with a dragon on the front.

'And I thought you was going to kill me,' said Anne. 'You look the most unlikely person to kill anyone.'

'I can't solve the matter,' said Emmett, 'if people don't tell me things.'

'Until I know you're kosher, until I know I can trust you, I won't pass anything on. I don't hold it here,' said Anne. 'What I have is hidden away. You might be genuine. You might just be an officer doing your duty. God knows there's enough of you to do that. But the heavy-handed ones, the ones that it matters to, the ones who are dodgy, they'll take the information from you and then they'll take the life from me. So, no thanks. You're welcome to your coffee. But I'm not giving you anything else.'

Emmett thanked her, drank up his coffee, and motioned for Sabine to follow him. As they got back into the car, Sabine asked him where to go.

'Let's go find a hotel. Let's stick around,' said Emmett.

'Some more people you want to see?'

'We don't seem to be getting any information from our two primary contacts. But I wonder who knows that.'

'What do you mean?' asked Sabine.

'We've been to two opposite sides of the story, you could say. One was a policeman, the other one was the press's man. We might have opposite sides here. They might wonder who's told who what. Let's pitch camp, see if anyone comes to us.'

Chapter 05

Emmett picked an old-style hotel in Pitlochry, towards the edge of the town. It had thick walls, without modern insulation, but the windows had been replaced with an up-to-date equivalent. There was certainly enough heat blasting through the hotel to keep away the snowy visage outside.

The trappings and trimmings were old-style: long curtains, tartan here and there, and proper carpets on the floors. There was, however, a modernness to it as well, with each room having its TV, and a proper power shower. Emmett appreciated the effort to change it from what looked like a 1980s building into a modern-day hotel. Their rooms were just down the corridor from each other.

Having booked in, Emmett went for a shower and a change before meeting Sabine for dinner. He knocked on her door dressed in his blue jeans and a dice t-shirt that she'd bought him at one of the comic cons he'd attended. When she opened the door, he couldn't help but force a smile that she too was in her blue jeans and one of the t-shirts he bought her at the comic cons. They looked at each other.

'Would you have been offended if I'd worn something else?'

asked Sabine. 'Because sometimes I think we try too hard.'

Emmett stared at her, and she saw the little smile on his face.

'Let's get something to eat,' he said.

The pair walked side by side down the corridor, Sabine slightly taller, and Emmett gave way to another couple passing down the other way. There was something else about him that always hit Sabine. He was well-mannered, and he had told her it was because of his mother. If a man couldn't be well-mannered towards a woman, how would he treat her when things got rough? It was funny, though, because Emmett showed no signs of wanting to have a woman in his life.

Sabine stopped herself. Well, he wanted a friend, not a woman. That's why she was in his life, not just a colleague.

The restaurant was only half full, this not being the busiest time of year, and they were seated in a corner. Emmett ordered steak and chips while Sabine went for a fish course.

As they sat to eat, they discussed the current changes that had gone within one of their role-playing games. Emmett didn't like to discuss a case over food. He had to switch off. In fact, he was insistent about this.

'If you ask me,' said Sabine—and I know I haven't been doing these games as long as you have—it's just over-complicating things. It's just making it more awkward for more people to get involved.'

'But it makes it more realistic,' said Emmett. 'You can get monsters now that act like proper monsters. They're not just generically reduced to something small.'

Sabine always wondered if anybody had a clue what he was talking about. How would the conversation seem to anyone else on a nearby table?

'Don't look round now,' said Emmett, 'but I think we're being

35

watched and listened to.'

Sabine didn't take her eyes off Emmett. 'Where?' she asked.

'About three o'clock off your left shoulder,' he said.

'Well, if you ask me,' she said, 'I don't see how you can really add a gorgon to a manticore.'

Emmett gave a grin, for he knew what she was doing, and was more than happy with it. They had to keep the conversation going, as if it was their normal one, but at some point, she would look round and clock the man Emmett had noted.

Sabine turned about a minute and a half later, with a quick glance.

It was a man on his own. He had a briefcase off to one side and was making just too much effort at being a businessman. Not that he was looking over at them, because people on their own when they dine will look around them. It was almost as if he was looking over at only them, as if he was in earshot.

You got to choose your tables here, and he was sitting at an awkward one. Not one you would walk up to naturally. You would go to one corner, go to the side. He was sitting where he could listen in casually.

'Do you want another drink?' asked Emmett.

'Yes,' said Sabine. 'I'll get them, though.'

'Don't be absurd. I will get them.'

'Do you know what really annoys me about you?' said Sabine. 'You get guys who treat a woman really nice because they're trying to get in with them. You just do it because that's what you're meant to do. Treat people nice for their sake, not your own. You're too nice, do you know that? A girl wouldn't know when you were being special to them.'

With that, she stood up and saw the look on Emmett's face.

'What?' she said. 'They wouldn't. How would any girl know when you were being special to them?'

'I'd probably let them paint some of my models,' he blurted. Sabine turned away, stifling a laugh.

She knew he wasn't being funny. He was deadly serious. If you actually got to handle the models, if you actually got to paint them. She walked over towards the bar. It suddenly dawned on her. He had actually let her paint one or two. They were some of the basic ones, extras, copies he had. Nothing special. Or had he meant it to be? Or was he just being honest?

Sabine ordered a couple more drinks and turned round to look back to where Emmett was sitting. He had his head down now, but she glanced across to the man who had been watching them. He was taking photographs. It was subtle, very subtle, using the mobile phone in front of him he was pretending to scroll through. But he wasn't, he was taking photographs.

A few minutes later, Sabine sat down, and they continued to eat the last of their dinner. A waitress arrived to clear the plates away, noticed the second set of glasses, and advised that she could come and get drinks at any time. Sabine knew this, but she had to see if the man was watching them.

'If you want to know if a man wants you,' said Emmett, 'maybe he should just invite you to his room.'

Sabine looked at him, shocked. 'I'm sorry?' she said.

'It might be better if they went to her room, though.'

He reached forward with his hands, grabbing hers and pulled them close. He leaned forward, looking up into her eyes. 'We're away, miles from anyone. Let's do it. You know I've always wanted you. Let's do it. Right now. Stuff dessert,' he said.

Sabine stared at him. Her heart skipped a beat.

37

What was he doing? Was he being genuine? He couldn't be being genuine. All this time? He was at something, wasn't he? He must be . . .

But Emmett was on his feet, and he hadn't let go of one of her hands. Suddenly, she was up on her feet too, and he was almost half running out of the restaurant. As she exited through the doors, shouting at the waiters to put it on the hotel bill, she saw the man who'd been watching them stand up. He was a good six feet four, now that he was standing. His hands looked strong and rough, and he had a moustache. That was the last she saw of him, as Emmett dragged her along the hotel corridors.

'Your room,' said Emmett. 'Your room. Come on.'

They got to Sabine's door, and as she fumbled for a key pass, she saw the man come round the corner. Emmett instantly pushed her up against the wall, planted a kiss on her, and his hands began to roam. Her hands grabbed hold of him until they broke off and she breathlessly said, 'Inside.'

She tapped on the reader with the hotel pass. Emmett pushed open the door, and the two of them stepped inside. Sabine felt the blood pumping and then spun back to see Emmett up against the door, his ear close to it. His hand was up, and a finger was telling Sabine to wait.

For a few moments, Emmett stopped. And then he went over to the bed and began to jump on it.

'Let's see you!' he cried out loud. 'Oh, yes, yes!' he shouted. He turned to Sabine, his hands imploring that she say something.

'Oh!' she moaned. 'Oh!'

Emmett indicated she should come to the bed, and he motioned for her to roll around on it. As she did so, he made his way back to the door. Listening carefully, after a few minutes, he put his hand up again and walked over to the window of the room. He looked out. They were on the ground floor, and the window was more of a shutter, which he pushed up.

'Are you coming?' he said.

Sabine was looking at him in disbelief. 'What was all that for?' she asked.

'He needs to think we're at it. Come on.'

'Shouldn't I stay here in case he comes back?'

'If I get into a fight,' said Emmett, 'I want you there. You can handle your fists better than I can.'

And Emmett was away, climbing out the window. She heard him land on the snow outside. Emmett turned back to run along the side of the building and Sabine caught him going round the corner towards the front entrance. She legged it, following hard, aware that in her T-shirt and jeans, the biting cold was getting hold of her.

The rush of warm air as she stepped in through the front doors was welcome, but she couldn't stop. Emmett was going as quick as he could through the hotel corridors until they got back to their own one. She caught up with him just as he arrived at his own room door. It looked shut and locked, just as Emmett had left it.

Emmett held up his hand, indicating that the man would be inside. He reached down and took out his room key. There was a faint whir as the room unlocked. Emmett pushed the handle down, pushed open the door, and raced in quickly.

Sabine followed, and they saw a man on the far side of the room. The room had a double bed in it, a desk in the far corner, and a TV opposite the bed. On top of the desk was a file, now lying open, pages everywhere. Emmett was making to go for the man, but the man spun quickly, and Sabine saw a weapon being pulled.

She dived at Emmett's feet, tripping him and sending him sprawling to the floor. She was waiting for the bang, for the crack of gunfire. None came. Instead, she heard somebody run across the bed and then land behind them, before running out the door. She rolled and got up to go after them. She heard a cry from Emmett.

'Wait,' he said. 'Don't.'

'But he'll get away,' said Sabine.

'Yes, he will. I think he's police.'

'What?' said Sabine. 'What do you mean he's police?'

'I think he's police. He pulled a weapon, but he didn't fire. He may not be in the force, but he's working for someone within it. Someone who knows that bloodshed makes things worse.'

Emmett stood up, walked over, and closed the door while Sabine tried to wind down.

'Sit down on the bed,' said Emmett as he went to the window. Satisfied, after looking out, he turned and pulled up the chair from beside the desk.

'He wants to know what you're at,' said Sabine. 'He's come looking for your stuff.'

'That's what I thought. We've been sent down here by Macleod. They know that. They know Macleod set up a cold case unit. Macleod could never come back and investigate this.

'They'd be worried about him. There's something to cover up. There's something to hide. Anne Matthews knows something, but we can't find out what. But they know we were there. They know we've been to Isbister's wife, Isabelle, and her new husband. They know we're investigating. But they don't know what Anne Matthews told us. So they've come to find out. Come to see our notes.'

'Well, they've had a darn good look. Not that we could tell them anything, because she didn't tell us anything.'

'No, but they didn't know that.'

'But they do now,' said Sabine.

'No, they don't. Give us a hand picking this stuff up,' said Emmett. He went down on his knees to pick the paper up off the floor, all the sheets that had been inside the folder that had been opened by the intruder.

Sabine joined him and as she picked one up, she could see an orc across part of the page. There were some pictures of dice. There was a table explaining how to roll for stamina and for dexterity. She laughed.

'Don't think it's funny. You've got to get this back in order. I was using this,' said Emmett.

Sabine understood she was looking at the new rules for Emmett's role-playing games. He had been studying them and had placed them into the file, knowing someone would come.

'You seriously left it on the table. They will not buy that.'

'It was underneath in the drawer,' said Emmett.

'You played that well,' said Sabine. 'I nearly got worried when you grabbed me at the table.'

Emmett looked at her. 'Why?' he said.

Sabine shook her head. 'Not to worry. Where does this leave us, though?'

'This leaves me wanting to talk to my boss,' said Emmett. 'We've definitely got one side that wants us to stop looking into this, or at least understand what we know. But if there's one side stopping it, you've also got Anne Matthews looking to expose it. Has Anne Matthews got an army? Has she got other people backing her? We don't know.'

'So we go back to Anne,' said Sabine.

'No,' said Emmett, 'we go to the one person who wants the same thing as her. We go to Macleod. He needs to talk to me about what's really going on here.'

Chapter 06

Emmett stood outside the car as the snow continued to fall. He was wearing a beanie hat with a gaming convention logo across the front. It was complimented by a large jacket, one worn by bin men when they were working the lorries in the bitter cold. He had produced it from the boot of the car, separate to his bomber jacket.

Emmett was also in thermal trousers, with thick boots on underneath. Standing a good thirty metres away, inside a bus station shelter, was Sabine. She had so many clothes on, Emmett wasn't sure it was still her.

Then he saw her nose protruding out, the curve of her lips and her chin. He reckoned it must have been her hair; it was covered with the hat she was wearing, her eyes by the glasses, and thick gloves covered her hands. For all of this, she was still moving around consistently, feeling the cold. Emmett stood in the car park, a little-known one, somewhere in the Cairngorms.

He'd chosen the place because anyone coming up here at this time was either who he wanted to meet or would be watching them. The area was a large bowl, and you could see the surrounding countryside easily.

It had shaken him that the intruder had been carrying a gun. Private detectives rarely did that. Policemen didn't do that. Even criminals, if they were following you and breaking in, might have stashed something heavy to attack you with. But to have a gun meant you could use it. It wasn't just there for a threat.

Emmett didn't like guns. Too easy to wield. Hit somebody with a bar, and you heard it crack the bone and saw the blood run from the head injury. Unless you were intent on seriously damaging them, you thought twice about the second hit. With a gun, often there was only one shot needed.

He heard the car before he saw it but the lights cut through the snow as it turned into the car park. Slowly it pulled up beside him and a window rolled down.

'I think Sabine's feeling it already. And if I go inside the car, she will not be happy with me,' said Emmett. 'Besides, I think if you're more comfortable, you'll be better at covering up what you want to tell me and what you don't.'

'What's the matter?' asked Macleod, emerging from his vehicle. 'You got spooked because somebody came after you?'

'They didn't come after us,' said Emmett. 'They wanted to know what we were doing. And I want to know what we're doing as well.'

'How do you mean?' asked Macleod.

'Tell me everything about Isbister.'

Macleod stared at Emmett for a moment. He turned away, his hands flexing in their black gloves.

'Orca,' said Macleod, 'was a man I barely knew. I knew him as a colleague. We'd done a couple of cases in Glasgow, and he was competent. Very competent. Good detective. One of the ones known for being trustworthy. Even the criminals said that about him. He wouldn't mess them about, and that wasn't always the case. Certain policemen like to take charge, dominate the criminals.'

'Do you?'

Macleod raised his eyebrows. 'I like to get the evidence, catch them, and put them away.'

'So, what happened?'

'I got assigned to the team in Glasgow. I was still quite young—hadn't long moved down from the Isle of Lewis after I'd lost my wife. Orca was a decent colleague, a decent friend. When I got to know him, he'd spoken, not directly but hinted at corruption in the team, but he was warning me not to go higher, warning me to watch out for myself.'

'I was still very naïve back then. We were the police; we were the good guys. Why would I be looking for anything like that? And then I thought he was a conspiracy theorist. He talked about things, but not in any detail. So, I thought he just saw things that weren't there. I had no evidence to the contrary. We got sent up to Pitlochry.

'Ian McCollum was dead. Somebody had killed him. It was clear that Simon Matthews had been in contact with him. They'd been seen frequently. Together, quietly, out of the way. Simon Matthews had a chequered history with the police, causing them trouble. Some of my superiors said he was a troublemaker, tied into the gangs.

'Stu McIntosh's gang at the time were big, very big! Tough to take down. People didn't speak, as they were so afraid of him. Then Ian McCollum died. Who would have taken him out? We couldn't find any decent leads except for Simon Matthews and his dealings with McCollum. This was all reported back. We

45

were about to go further, and I got whipped back to Glasgow to look at a different murder.

'It was fairly run-of-the-mill, a domestic,' continued Macleod. 'Solved it in three days. I went to come back up and they said no. Directed me elsewhere when there weren't things happening. Of course, by this time Matthews was dead; Isbister was implicated. They'd found a knife with his fingerprints on it beside Matthews.

'And then, Orca never came back. The suicide note was picked up, too. Came from the wife.'

'They directly stopped you from going up to investigate?' asked Emmett.

'No. Not directly in that sense. Wasn't an order. It was a quiet talking to. It wouldn't be good. I was tied in with Isbister so I shouldn't be there. There was no blame on me. I'd just come into the unit. They didn't see me as being compromised. But they said for me to investigate someone I was working with wouldn't be sensible. So, I gave a brief statement. And that was it.'

'The thing was,' said Macleod, 'Stu McIntosh's gang disappeared off the Glasgow map. I investigated several murders, all described as gangland killings, but there was nobody that came up to take over the void. When you have a gangland area like that, someone will try to take over,' said Macleod.

'They'd step in; they'd seize whatever was going on—the drugs, extortion, the brothels that were running. It took too long for them to be filled. Something wasn't right. But I couldn't get back to investigate.'

'It doesn't seem like you,' said Emmett. 'You're very determined, very driven.'

'I am now,' said Macleod. 'My wife had died. I was in

Glasgow to get away from that. My whole being had been destroyed, Emmett,' said Macleod. Emmett could see he was shaking now. 'That time of my life was some of the darkest days I have been through. You didn't know me until Inverness.

'When I was in Glasgow, I was a hard man. Not in the sense of beating people. I thought Hope was some sort of floozy, or worse, when I first worked with her.'

Emmett stared at him. 'Why?'

'I came from a religious background that said you knew your place, you had to be in it, and women certainly did not wear the likes of what they wear today. Even Sabine there, she wears nothing that's not appropriate, modest. But where I came from, you didn't even wear stuff like that. And women knew their place, and their place was at home.

'I had my Hope. My first wife. She wasn't like that. She had broken me out of that mould to a large degree. And then she was gone. I didn't know what to do. And I fell back on what I had been brought up with. I fell on it hard. And I failed as best I could because of it. Today, I wouldn't have let them do that to me. I would have run round the houses to have solved it. But not then. And now there's no time. And if I get involved now, or look like it's me, they'll raise merry hell. But you, they don't know.'

'So what? You stuck me into this? You just threw me in? A vendetta or a personal crusade of yours?'

'Justice is not a personal crusade,' said Macleod.

'But why now?'

'Why not?' countered Macleod.

'When Stu McIntosh's gang was killed, didn't you see a pattern? Didn't you see?'

'Understand,' said Macleod. 'There was no common SIO.

47

No common person investigating. No one person you could accuse of covering everything up. It was bits and pieces. You couldn't get near it. Everything looked like it should have. Beaten up, killed, dumped in a back alley. It was classic gangland. There were even markings put on from other gangs. But when I went to the other gangs, I saw the shock, saw the horror, because you didn't mess with McIntosh in those days.

'The other gangs were smaller. He was dominating. He was taking over the entire city. And then he didn't. He was taken out. When I came down to Glasgow,' said Macleod, 'Orca helped me. He was a friend. Not a close friend, but he was a good colleague, and he was a decent officer.

'They didn't just kill him, they took away his name. And I don't know if he committed suicide. I don't know if somebody got rid of him, because so many people were got rid of then.'

'But why now?' said Emmett. 'Again, I ask, why now?'

'I've never had the influence,' said Macleod. 'I've never been able to do it. I couldn't investigate it as part of my job. You can. It's a cold case.'

'It doesn't really fit in, though, does it? And to what point? To what purpose?'

'Justice,' said Macleod.

'But this is wrapped up. All that this case says is we don't know where he committed suicide. He's not shown his face once since,' said Emmett. 'And if I find him somewhere, what then? Do we bring it all back up? This is not something that should be chased at the moment. Why am I doing this now?'

'Because I let him down,' said Macleod. 'And you? Well.'

'You want me to believe,' said Emmett, 'that I am taking this case because you let Isbister down. It has bugged you for all of your career and you've now got an opportunity to do it. So, you've turned round and thrown me straight in with this?'

'You can believe what you want,' said Macleod. 'I didn't put you on these cases to be told how to run them or how to do it. I give my detectives latitude. Clarissa isn't Hope. Hope isn't you. You're very different. I need another set of eyes on the case.'

Emmett turned away for a moment. 'The next time I call you to me,' said Emmett, 'can you promise me something?'

'What?' asked Macleod.

'That you don't give me a bit of the truth. You give me the whole thing? Because nobody's telling me anything about this at the moment. And that's bothering me. But it's also bothering me because you're placing my colleague in danger.'

'Sabine can handle herself,' said Macleod. 'Clarissa said she always could.'

'It doesn't matter if she can handle herself or not. We shouldn't put her in harm's way if we don't need to. We all should know what we're walking into.'

'I let him down. It's certainly one reason. Find out what happened.'

Macleod turned away, opened the car door and got inside. After a minute, he started the car and drove off. Sabine walked over to Emmett.

'Useful?' asked Sabine.

'Is there anybody watching?'

'Not that I could see. The old man's not daft either. He'd have picked up on it. He's probably checked around the area before he came.'

'You're right there,' said Emmett. 'The old man's not daft. What is he up to with this?'

'Did he not tell you the truth?'

49

'Not all of it,' said Emmett. 'In the car. Come on. I'll bring you up to speed.'

Chapter 07

'Do you really think that the McIntoshes will tell us anything?'

'I don't know,' said Emmett, in reply to Sabine's question. She was giving a little shake of her head, as if she wasn't sure if this was a good idea.

'It's a rough crowd. I know they're gone now.'

'Well, a lot of the key elements are gone, but you just don't become violent people. We want to be careful—what we ask, how we ask. I need their side of the story,' said Emmett. 'I need to understand what was happening. Simon Matthews. From what I can tell, he was a decent person. Not liked because he dug up the muck. Authorities wouldn't like what he would highlight.'

'Do you think what they tell us will be true?' asked Sabine.

'Well, what have they got to lose? If they talk to us at all?'

'They could be worried that we're there to make sure old things are thoroughly covered up.' Anne Matthews didn't believe we were there to do good.'

'Anne Matthews is in a very vulnerable position,' said Emmett. 'Sitting between the McIntoshes and ourselves. She's still in Pitlochry. As she said herself, still there to find out what really happened to her husband. That's a dangerous woman. One who'll be watched. I fully understand why she wouldn't talk to us. She didn't know who we were. She talked about Macleod coming.'

'It'd be a lot easier if he did,' said Sabine.

The hills around Glasgow were full of snow. As they descended towards the city and the mass of traffic that was the M8 in the early hours of the morning, Sabine thought Emmett looked a little edgy. He wasn't one for conflict. He was an excellent officer, but he wasn't the action type. It was why they complimented each other well. Sabine wasn't afraid of things getting rough. She could handle herself. She always could. Emmett wasn't that way inclined.

He was too nice. Too ready to see other people's side of the world. But that's what made him a good detective. He could see everyone's side of the world. Sabine wondered if it was the roleplay that helped him with that. Having to get in character, having to take up a stance from a character's point of view. When he ran as a games master for his roleplaying groups, he had to be several characters in those games.

Ellen McIntosh lived in the West End of Glasgow, close to Byres Road. Her house wasn't as salubrious as one might have thought, given that her husband had at one point dominated the criminal landscape across Glasgow. But it wasn't a cheap area either.

Sabine turned off the M8 and slowly plodded along the wide roads with the tall buildings on either side. She found herself glad that she'd moved north. Sabine was a country girl deep down. She liked to be out walking—a physical girl who enjoyed the fresh air around her face. Sure, she could dress up when she had to. She could look the part. But deep down, she wanted the wildness. She glanced over at Emmett, who was staring out of the window.

'Bit of a come down,' said Emmett. 'I heard once they had quite a large estate outside of Glasgow. They bought it at their height. Had to sell it. Debts, lawyers' fees, things like that.'

'Still quite a pricey area she's in, though, isn't it?'

'Pricey area,' said Emmett. 'And not that far from what remains of their firm for protection.' He said it with a deep thoughtfulness and almost hinted at a slight fear.

'We're just going to talk,' said Sabine.

'I know. Just take it easy, though. Be your charming self,' said Emmett.

After turning off the principal streets through the West End, Sabine parked up in front of a house that was now four different flats.

There were gardens around it, all covered in snow, and their feet crunched as they made their way to the front door. She pressed on the buzzer that said McIntosh. Sabine never wondered how other people felt living with the wife of one of Glasgow's most notorious criminals.

'Yes?' said a voice from the door communications system.

'Hello, I'm here to speak to Ellen McIntosh. This is Acting DI Emmett Grump.'

'Piss off, copper.'

'I'm not here to arrest you, not here to go after speeding tickets, or anything else. I'm here to talk about Stu and possible police collusion.'

Sabine glanced over at Emmett. He raised his shoulders. 'Potential,' he said under his breath. 'Just potential. Got to get her down somehow.'

The speaker switched off and after a moment, steps could

be heard coming down the stairs inside. The door opened and a man, maybe in his forties, stared out. He was strong looking, with tattoos down the side of his face.

'You Grump?' he said.

'Acting DI Emmett Grump. This is Detective Sergeant Sabine Ferguson. We'd like to talk to Ellen McIntosh.'

'You don't upset her, all right. Don't piss her about; otherwise, you can just get the hell out.'

'I'm not here to upset people,' said Emmett. 'I'm here to find something out. The truth.'

'You'll be the first bloody copper who did. Go on. Up the stairs. First on the left.'

'You're not coming with us?' asked Emmett.

'Why? Do you need a bloody escort?'

Emmett shrugged his shoulders. Followed by Sabine, he trudged up the stairs. It was a wide staircase, and the house had once all been one. Now it was split up into flats, with prices realised that were so much more.

Emmett rapped on the door at the top, and it was opened by another tough looking man. He might have been the man's brother from downstairs. The tough man pointed to a door and Emmett opened it to see a woman sitting in a chair on the far side. She was thin, with black hair down to her shoulders, but she must have been late sixties if not seventies. Her hands were bony and, while probably attractive back in the day, there was a hardness about her face. Her nose was large but pointed, and the lines down her neck told of many years under pressure.

'Spit it out, Grump,' said the woman. 'I don't entertain fools.'

'Good,' said Emmett. 'Your husband was Stu McIntosh. Hard criminal empire. Taken down in two years. Lots of murders from unknown people. Don't seem right.'

'Of course it wasn't right. They came after him, didn't they? Your bloody lot. Don't you know that?'

'I don't know that, but I need to know. I'm looking into the death, or suspected death, of DC Isbister.'

The woman looked up at Emmett. 'From what point of view?' she asked.

'Doesn't make sense to me what's going on. I work up in Inverness now on a cold case unit. I've been instructed to look into this case.'

'Why would they want to look into it? Open and closed case. We lost Ian up there. Pitlochry. He was the first. They killed him. They killed Stu afterwards down the line, but not before they'd taken out all of his buddies. Your lot did it. So I don't buy it. Why would you be opening this up? There's no way they would pull a file on this. This would stay buried. Even somebody who wanted the truth would keep this buried. There's too much scandal, loss of public face. You, and your type, don't win opening this up.'

'My boss is DCI Macleod. He was on the case before they took him off it, before Simon Matthews died and Isbister disappeared. Isbister was a colleague of his.'

'Macleod,' said Ellen. She stood up and walked over to the window. 'This is it, you know. This is my view now. We had a lovely place just outside the city, on the up. When they brought it down, they never found out most of what we were up to. They never closed the rackets properly. They just went out and killed them, one by one, until people wouldn't work for us. We weren't a good bet. We weren't safe to work for. Nobody was taking over. Do you understand that? It must have been your lot,' she said.

Ellen turned and walked over to a cabinet, pulled a pack of

cigarettes out from it, and lit one. She drew hard, drawing in the smoke before blowing it out.

'Macleod was the only one that got close. He shut down a couple of operations, but he didn't get involved in our murders. Never involved when one of ours went down.'

'Simon Matthews?' said Emmett. 'He was talking to Ian Cullen. That's why Macleod fingered him as a potential suspect. I don't think Macleod thought he did anything, and then he turned up dead after Macleod was taken off the case. A couple of days later, Isbister was fingered for it.'

'Simon Matthews was on to your lot. You know that, don't you?' said Ellen. 'He spoke to Stu a few days beforehand. Stu had lost several key henchmen, and he lost McCollum too, when he sent him up there to speak to Matthews. Matthews wanted to highlight everything. He was a scandal maker, someone who wanted to revel in being able to show the chaos. He was a way in for Stu, to work out who was coming after us.'

'He didn't come to you then because he had something on you?' asked Sabine.

'Had something on us? He would have been insane. To come and tell Stu he had something on us. Stu would have killed him. Stu would have buried him somewhere. And he would have made a flag of it to tell everyone else; you don't come after me. But people were. Someone was coming after my Stu. Someone was killing his henchmen. And Matthews had an idea.

'Ian McCollum was up there to talk to him,' continued Ellen. 'And then Ian was dead before he could tell us anything. And then Macleod and Isbister were up there. You guys were all over it. We couldn't get near it, but he wanted Matthews, did my Stu. My Stu wanted Matthews. He wanted him, and he was going to extract whatever information he had in him. They weren't buddies; they weren't friends; we weren't working off the same page.

'But Matthews, for all that, he was a little weasel digging in and finding out and infiltrating—he knew something and Stu wanted to know, too. He had an idea who was coming after us, and if Stu had found out, he'd have gone for them and killed them. He'd have declared open war.'

'Or he might have got Matthews to just make it all very public. That would have been a good one,' said Emmett.

'He'd have killed somebody for it,' said Ellen. She walked over and stood in front of a picture on the wall. The man in it was wearing a Scotland shirt with tattoos all the way down his arm. Images of Scotland proudly displayed and red hair with a red beard. He had a stomach to match. Big and round. But he looked fearsome.

'He was the gentlest of men with me,' said Anne. ' And trust me, I had some before him who weren't gentle. He looked after me. I'm still looked after. Taught his boys to do that too.'

'Where would I go to find out what Matthews knew? Is there anybody else?' asked Emmett. 'Anywhere else I can go to dig up those secrets?'

'If I could have dug them up, I'd have dug them up. Stu would have dug them up back then. Whatever Matthews knew died with him. And they came after us. Isbister probably killed him. He's probably sitting on a beach somewhere. Far, far away. Happy. Living it up.'

'He left his wife. She's still mourning him. She's still trying to work out what happened to him,' said Sabine.

'Bitch probably got paid off,' said Ellen.

'No,' said Sabine. 'I've met her. She's like you.' Ellen glanced over, eyes almost like daggers. 'She loved her man in that way. And like you, if she could find out, she'd find out.'

Ellen took another drag on her cigarette.

'Well, that's your story. You want to find out what happened to us? Want to find out who was silencing us? You'd better talk to your own. No criminals came for us. Whoever put Matthews in the ground was one of yours? Was it Isbister? I couldn't tell you. Reckon he's on a beach somewhere. I reckon he's lolling it up with a couple of teen girls around him. Paid for by your people.'

'I think you're wrong,' said Emmett. 'If I find out, I'll let you know.'

Emmett went to turn away. But Ellen shouted after him. 'Be careful if you go into this,' she said. 'My Stu, lovely to me, was a bastard to everyone else. He was brutal. He was ruthless. And they gutted his organisation. Look at you and your jeans. You don't even look the part. She looks more the part,' said Ellen, nodding at Sabine.

'But even you, dear. They'd take you apart, and take you both down. And don't bother coming back to me. I don't care no more. Can't bring him back. He left me well off. If I try to find out what happened to him, I'll probably be in a grave.'

Ellen shouted, and the door opened. One of the large men entered. 'Acting DI Grump is leaving,' said Ellen.

'Thank you for your time,' said Emmett. He strode off down the stairs, followed by Sabine, tailed all the way by the large man. The front door was opened by the supposed brother, and when they got back to the car, Sabine turned the engine on quickly. She looked over at Emmett. His hands were shaking.

'You okay?' she said.

'Well, that could have gone a lot worse. I reckon she was responsible for at least five deaths. I looked it up.' He gave a smile and then looked out the window again. Sabine drove off.

Chapter 08

Sabine Ferguson dropped Emmett at a coffee shop while she headed back to the Glasgow station where her former arts team had been based. There were still some items she had to clear out and as she was over this way, it was a good time to pick them up. She had enjoyed her time on the Arts team, but they were very much the add-on in the station.

That being said, Sabine was fairly popular. She realised from some men this was because she had a figure to look at. Others enjoyed her bright disposition and her Northern Irish wit, but she was also amenable. They also knew she was someone who could help if she was asked.

Snow was falling heavily as she pulled into the car park at the rear of the station. Stepping out of the car, she saw someone she thought she knew. PC Emma MacKay. She'd walked the beat with Sabine once. But while Sabine had moved up to sergeant, Emma now had two children and was still working as a constable. Despite this, they'd remained on good terms when they'd met in the station. And Sabine was always happy to see her.

'Emma!' shouted Sabine through the blowing snow.

'Sergeant,' said Emma. The woman was small compared to

Sabine, with long blonde hair that was tied up.

She was dressed for work, coming in on the afternoon shift, but her face showed only hostility.

'How are things?' asked Sabine, wondering what was up.

'Things are fine. If you don't mind, I need to get on.'

'Okay. How's Timothy?' asked Sabine, referring to her first child.

'Fine,' said Emma and headed off, almost running ahead of Sabine, into the building. When Sabine entered the building, she caught a look from several officers walking past. A couple didn't look at her at all, but then she didn't recognise their faces. But others, those who should have known her, met her either with hard stares or simple-blank faces.

Sabine took a side turn into the canteen, took a cup of coffee, and sat down. Usually in the Glasgow station, somebody you would know would pop by and sit with you and have a chat. And not having been there for a short while, Sabine thought someone would join her soon enough. She saw several people who should have, but they stopped at different tables far away from her. Was she smelling bad today? What was going on? Had something happened Sabine wasn't aware of?

Sabine finished her coffee, and went to stand up when Sergeant Angela Breckin sat beside her.

She was a dark-haired woman, very thin, with bony cheeks and the pair of them had once sat sergeant exams together. She wasn't the warmest of people, being blunt and direct, always prepared to tell you what she was thinking of you. There were no hidden doors with Angela. Everything was as you got.

'Surprised you're here.'

'I'm just clearing out,' said Sabine. 'How are you, anyway?'

'Running it thin talking to you.'

'How do you mean?' asked Sabine.

'Checking up on us. On the murder team. What's Macleod got against Glasgow now?'

'I'm working cold case out of Inverness.'

'Cold case on a Glasgow murder squad. One of Macleod's old teams. What's he digging up? Heard rumours you're trying to vindicate the McIntoshes,' spat Angela.

'Vindicate the McIntoshes?'

'Well, you've been there, haven't you? What's all that about, then?'

'Whoa,' said Sabine. 'I like you, Angela, but you don't get to throw accusations like that at me.'

'Get yourself back out of here. You will not find yourself very welcome. You don't turn on people like that.'

'I haven't turned on anyone,' said Sabine.

'Looking at Isbister. That was a dark day. That doesn't need brought up,' said Angela. 'Everyone knows what Isbister was.'

'Do you?' said Sabine, almost shocked by her own vehemence. 'Do you really? Does anyone? Well, actually someone does. Some people here do know.'

'The bad egg. Bad times. Not something to be brought up and you certainly don't want to defend the McIntoshes. Those bastards killed some of ours.'

'I work for Macleod. Macleod is no bad egg,' said Sabine. 'If you don't know that, you don't know the man at all.'

She stood up and walked out, leaving Angela behind her. Rather than see anyone, Sabine made her way directly to clear out her old locker, where she had stowed some of her equipment. As she opened it up, she noted that several of the constables who were kicking about left the room.

Sabine felt an icy chill, and she was bemused at the entire

attitude towards her. She turned and looked down the line of the lockers to see a woman step out from behind them. The woman was shorter than Sabine, but she was a big woman. She wore a long skirt and had a jacket wrapped around her.

'I don't think I know you,' said the big woman. 'But clearly other people do. You've cleared this place in no time. . . . You look like one of his crowd. He always did like the good-looking birds.'

'He likes the competant detectives,' spat Sabine.

'Is that why he's got Cunningham on board? Somebody told me she was the Inverness bike.'

'I'm not sure I like your tone,' said Sabine. 'Who the hell are you, anyway?'

'DCI Harlow. And I need a word in your ear.'

'I've got my mobile,' said Sabine. 'You want to talk to Macleod? Tell him. You can tell DI Grump.'

'Acting DI Grump. That little gobshite. He was a weirdo. No wonder Macleod picked him to do this.'

Sabine's blood was boiling. She wanted to stroll down the line of lockers and plant one on this woman. But she was a DCI, so Sabine would have to be careful.

'Just say it then,' said Sabine. 'Just say why you've turned this entire station against me. Just tell me why when I was a perfectly happy sergeant here who could talk to everyone. Apart from the new people, I can't get a look from anyone. It's only the people that don't know me that aren't staring with anger.'

'Some things need to be left to lie,' said Harlow.

She was wearing a dark green bucket hat. Harlow took it off and placed it on the bench beside her. Her hair was down to her shoulders, but it was fading and thin. *She must be around*

Macleod's age, thought Sabine.

'Isbister was a bad egg. An egg that was cracked and needs to lie, and needs to not come back.'

'Why?' asked Sabine.

'Because Isbister tried to adjust things, tried to make things happen on his own. Didn't listen, didn't do the right thing.'

'It's funny,' said Sabine. 'According to my boss, he never clocked that. Macleod says he was a fine copper. Orcadian, nice man.'

'Macleod barely knew him; didn't know how to get in behind him. We worked with Orca for a lot longer. Orca was a whale that needed harpooning.'

'But we never got to him. What happened to him?' asked Sabine, walking down the corridor towards DCI Harlow who was now sitting on the bench. She wasn't cutting the damning figure she originally had.

'Committed suicide, didn't he?'

'Did he?' asked Sabine, coming up close now.

DCI Harlow waved her hands. 'That was the tale. That was the note that was left.'

'But is that what happened to him?' asked Sabine.

'No.'

'So where is he?'

'I don't know,' said Harlow. 'An old grass helped Isbister get away, and that's why you can't dig it up. At the moment, he's a suicide. He saw the wrong of his ways. A corrupt police, a policeman that had to end himself. One who took down a valiant crusader who was highlighting what Isbister was. Macleod was Isbister's partner, albeit for a brief time. He doesn't want to bring this up either. He shouldn't. It'll taint him.'

'Since when was Macleod ever worried about being tainted?' asked Sabine. 'It's not his style, is it?'

'No, I grant you that. But back then, he didn't have that much riding on him. Look at what he's done in Inverness. The station. Clarissa Urquhart and her Arts team. That's where you came up. That's where you became something. Macleod is bringing on this new line of constables and sergeants.

'Hope McGrath, the glamour girl up there. Six-foot, red hair. Oh, the boys love her down here. Especially her arse in those jeans.'

Sabine clenched her fist. It was one thing when men spoke of a woman like that, but when another woman did it, it enraged Sabine. Hope had worked hard. Hope had fought to not be treated like some sort of model, to not be the glamour girl of the station. And here Harlow was throwing her to the wolves as one.

'Macleod won't sit back. He wants this discovered,' said Sabine. 'What happened to Isbister?'

'I told you I don't know. An old grass helped get him away.'

'Who would know? Let us go find him. If he's even still alive,' said Sabine.

'Keep it quiet, covered up. Keep it something that the public doesn't know. If they thought he got away . . . if they thought for a moment that he was still loose. Well . . .'

'Well, the McIntoshes wouldn't be happy, would they? Especially if McCollum was brought up there to—'

'Don't,' said Harlow. 'Don't think out any of it. Macleod wants an answer. Tell him. Tell him what you find. Go speak to Donald Mackey.'

'Donald Mackey? Who the hell's Donald Mackey?' asked Sabine.

'Mackey was a police informant. Macleod would have heard his name, though he didn't work with him. He's in Spain now. I'm sure you'll be resourceful enough to find him. He'll show you the current state of affairs. When he does, don't go any further. Tell Macleod that's what's happened. That's where the story ends. Go back to your glamorous lives up in Inverness, do some good police work and keep this nasty business away. Isbister is a rotten egg. If Macleod can't see that, he's not half the detective I thought he was,' said Harlow.

She stood up and put the hat on her head and looked at Sabine. 'Chose you too, didn't he? He likes his women.'

'He chose Clarissa Urquhart, and she chose me,' said Sabine. 'And I'll happily go up there and tell her your thoughts on our teams.'

The name Urquhart brought a reaction on Harlow's face. It was brief, momentary.

'Well, Urquhart chose you. I guess you must be all right. You're a reckless woman, though.'

Harlow went to walk off, but then she stopped and turned back.

'Grump, will he be a problem?' asked Harlow. 'I take it you can handle him. Heard when you two were down here that you spent a lot of time together. I wouldn't do that. It's never good when you work and sleep together.'

Sabine went to say it. They weren't sleeping together. They weren't an item. Hell, she wasn't going to give the satisfaction to Harlow that she was riled.

She watched Harlow disappear, heard the door close, and turned and punched the locker. It left a dent in some poor PC's locker. Sabine didn't care. She strode back to her own, lifted out the boxes that she had left there, and left the locker lying open. No one spoke to her as she left the building. She had spent a few years there, happy ones, and this treatment was biting at her.

Somehow, she was now seen as the enemy. Another part of her worried about how people saw Emmett and her. They were friends, and he was a good friend. She spun the wheel and drove out of the station car park into the Glasgow traffic. Emmett would be waiting. She wondered what he would say.

If he had been there, he'd have remained calm. He wouldn't have been worked up. And he wouldn't have batted an eyelid at the dig about her and him. *The trouble is,* thought Sabine, *I wouldn't have known if that was just because he was hiding his feelings, or if it was just his usual placid rejection of what others thought of him.*

A month or two ago, she would have said the latter. It worried her now that part of her hoped for the former.

Chapter 09

'So Alicante, here we come,' said Sabine. 'I didn't think you would just follow somebody's blunt hint like that. You know we're getting played.'

'I'm well aware of that, Sabine. But if we don't play the game, what have we got? Nowhere to go, nothing to dig up. They're selling us a story. But I'm assuming the story isn't true. Until we find out what isn't true about it, we won't know who's selling it.'

Sabine settled back in her seat as the plane rolled down the runway. Emmett looked completely distracted looking out of the window and this was probably some of the more awkward times she found with him.

When they'd gone out together to a gaming session, or even a comic con, he was deeply engaged, but when he was being a detective, he liked to think. He almost ignored his partner at times. It was taking a little bit of getting used to, for previously Sabine had been the one in charge and she'd simply gone to Emmett whenever she needed him. Now she felt sometimes she wasn't needed.

Maybe that was just the way he was. He was fonder of her than almost anyone else. That, she knew. He spent more time with her than anyone else. It was just that work had changed, and it seemed weird.

The roles were reversed. He was the one running this investigation, and yes, when he spoke to Macleod, he didn't exactly pander to him either. Previously, to run an investigation, he had gone to ask permission to take part in things. Clarissa wasn't someone you blanked and then turned around and told her what you did. He was also well out of his depth in the Arts field. He had to come to Sabine or Clarissa to understand any of the actual artwork. This style of detection in these cold cases was not something that Sabine was used to.

And yet she partly jumped on board because of Emmett. Yes, it would also help build her career. She needed to work in many departments. So from a career point of view, it was good. From a personal point of view, she got to work with her friend. Maybe that wasn't always the right thing.

'By the way,' said Emmett, almost absentmindedly, 'I told the Spanish police of our travel plans. Don't want them worried that two detectives have suddenly pitched up.'

'Were they bothered?'

'No. They gave me Donald Mackey's address. He's on the outskirts of Denia in Alicante. They were quite helpful in that sense. They just told me to get on with it, effectively, which is good.'

'I take it you packed something for warmer weather than what we've been having?'

'Threw a couple of t-shirts in. You?'

'Well, I wasn't sure how warm it would be. But I've got options.'

Emmett nodded. And Sabine knew he had no idea what any of those options would be. Nor did he really care.

Every now and again, he would just stare at her. Not in a provocative or a nasty way. She thought it was admiration. And if she did ask him, he would just say something like, 'You look good today. You look well. You're dressed pretty.' Something simple that didn't draw her into a conversation.

On arrival, they took a hire car from the airport, Sabine driving again, while Emmett sat pondering. It seemed to be a thing that if you were the boss, you never drove. Unless you were Clarissa in her car, of course. Nobody else got their hands on that little green car. Emmett gave directions.

As soon as the pair had arrived in Denia, they routed into a back street, where a small house was located amongst many others. It had high walls, with probably a little garden or courtyard inside, as was the way in the locality. Sabine rapped on a wooden gate door.

'Clear off,' said a voice.

Sabine banged again. 'We're looking for Donald Mackey.'

'Piss off,' said the voice.

'DCI Harlow sent us,' said Sabine.

She looked at Emmett, who simply gave a nod, approving of this idea. This time there was no response, but a few pattering steps told them someone was on the move. There was a click, and the wooden gate opened.

In front of them stood a man of average height. He had a worn face, big ears, and a large nose with grey, swept hair. He wore a basic polo shirt, but it looked like it hadn't been washed in days, and his cream chinos had coffee stains across the thighs. If Sabine closed her eyes, she would have sworn she was in a brewery; such was the stench that came from the man's mouth.

'Donald Mackey,' said Emmett. 'I'm Acting DI Emmett

Grump. This is Detective Sergeant Sabine Ferguson. We've been sent here to see Isbister.'

Donald Mackey, who had a flushed red colour when he opened the door, now went completely white. For a moment, he hesitated. And then he stepped back, offering a way into the house.

'Come in, come in; you must have a drink,' he said.

Emmett walked past, but Sabine knew that the man watched her closely as she walked up to his front door.

'It's open. Just go in,' he said, and followed closely behind Sabine. He was still pale as he reached for some drinks. Might not be what you're used to out here, but I've got some rum. Would you like some?'

'Not for me,' said Emmett, staring around the kitchen. It was simple, but had many cups and plates left lying around. Crumbs were everywhere, and the floor had muddy patches. A door at the rear of the kitchen led through to the rest of the house. The weather wasn't particularly warm, although for those who lived in Scotland, they would certainly appreciate the heat.

Mackey pointed to a chair, telling Sabine she could take that, and placed some rum down in front of her. She looked across at Emmett, who gave a nod, and Mackey placed himself in a seat directly opposite Sabine.

'So, what's the big deal?' asked Mackey. 'Isbister. You said Harlow sent you. I haven't seen Harlow in years. Strange she would get in touch now.'

'Maybe,' said Emmett, 'but they sent us out to try to find him. Maybe you could tell Sabine here what you know of him.'

'It's been a while,' said Mackey.

'We're trying to work out what happened to him,' said Sabine.

71

'Harlow said you would know. We asked Ellen McIntosh, but she didn't know.'

The mention of the name made Mackey go white again for a moment. But then he leaned forward and took Sabine's hand.

'Stay away from that woman. Bad news, the McIntoshes. I was good. I helped him, Isbister. He came to me and I got him away. It diffused the situation, you know?'

'Do you think we could know a little more about it?' asked Sabine. Mackey sat back, but his hand ran down across Sabine's thigh and then settled on her knee.

'I feel like you're someone I could talk to,' said Mackey.

Emmett looked across at Sabine from behind Mackey, gave her a nod, and quietly snuck out of the kitchen. He could hear Donald Mackey beginning to talk and Sabine's gentle voice encouraging the man. Emmet stood in a hallway before wandering through to a living room.

There was an old sofa, a television in the corner and a couple of empty bottles left lying around. The man was clearly a drunk. There were also some magazines scattered here and there. He left the living room and found a bedroom. The bed wasn't made and hadn't looked like it had been washed for several weeks. There were some girly magazines on the side, graphic in content, and pinned to the wall were some numbers.

Emmett checked them with his phone and the search engine reported they were escort agencies, particularly salubrious ones. The shower and bathroom were manky looking, and Emmett wondered did the man ever get a cleaner in.

He made his way through to another room. This one had a desk, a chair, and a laptop. There were a series of posters around the room, scantily clad women, but Emmett's eyes were drawn to the safe in the far corner. It looked old style with a dial and Emmett wondered how difficult it would be to pick it. However, beside the safe was a bin which Emmett delved into, pulling out several brown envelopes. The word 'rent' was on them.

So, is this his lifestyle? thought Emmett. *Is this what he was reduced to? Gone to Spain, broken and lonely. Buying girls to entertain him, while drinking himself silly. It would take money to do that. And he certainly didn't look like he would have a job. But who is paying the rent?*

Emmett took one envelope, placed it inside an evidence bag he had with him, and tucked it away in his pocket. He moved the mouse on the computer and the screen flashed up with another image of a naked woman.

Emmett used the mouse to highlight the gallery function and a spread of pictures came up on the screen. Some of them were women in various poses, some explicit, some were clearly images he'd liked off the web of good-looking women. But here and there were other images. Images that contained the same people. *Family*, thought Emmett, *family that aren't around anymore*. Emmett wondered. This was a man who could keep a secret, obviously—was paid to keep *something* under wraps. What that *something* was, wasn't entirely obvious.

Emmett walked back through to the kitchen, taking up a position behind Mackey again. Although Emmett couldn't see Mackey's face, he was sure he hadn't been missed. Donald Mackey was now leaning forward, close up to Sabine, and in fairness, she was letting him, aware that the man was clearly entranced to some degree.

When Sabine spoke to Mackey, she laughed, almost giggled. Emmett knew Sabine didn't do that. If Sabine liked you, as far as Emmett could tell, she spoke to you normally. She would be comfortable in your presence. He'd seen her in the Glasgow station, playing along with some officers there to get something out of them. She could flirt to a point, but only when she wanted something. She was playing Donald Mackey to a tee. Emmett noticed that the level of liquid in her glass hadn't reduced at all.

'Mr Mackey,' said Emmett. 'Do you know the whereabouts of Isbister?'

Mackey turned round and looked at him. 'Haven't you been listening at all?'

Behind him, Emmett saw Sabine pick up her glass and tip contents into a plant sitting across from her. By the time Mackey turned back to her, the glass was back in position.

'You need another one of those,' said Mackey and reached across for a bottle.

He knocked it but Sabine reached and caught it before it could tumble off the tabletop. 'I'll pour it,' she said, and put another shot in his glass before filling hers up.

'Can you take us to see Isbister?' asked Emmett again.

'You see, you,' said Mackey, pointing at Sabine. 'Lovely. You come in here; you talk to me like a proper human being. He is what we called back home, an arsehole.'

Emmett rolled his eyes. It was going to be like this, was it?

'Mr Mackey was saying he'll happily take us to see Isbister. Didn't you?' said Sabine, putting her hand on his now.

'Of course. I'll drive,' said Mackey. 'You can sit in the front with me,' he pointed at Sabine.

'I think not,' said Emmett. 'I think Sergeant Ferguson should drive us. You can sit in the front with her if you want.'

'Sabine,' said Mackey. 'Sabine, and I'm Donald. We're on first-name terms now. You—'

'Yes, Emmett,' said Sabine. 'Donald's going to help us.'

Sabine stood up and held her hand out for Donald. He almost half fell off his chair but rounded well enough to stand beside her.

'Better take your car,' he said. 'He doesn't want me to drive.'

Sabine was ushered in front of Donald, who clearly was enjoying the rear-view, and Emmett followed out behind him. At times, Donald looked unsteady, but Emmett noticed that whenever he had to, his feet found their footing rather easily. He wasn't sure how drunk the man was. He'd gone white when they'd arrived.

Was he playing them? If he wasn't, fair enough. But if he was, where was he taking them and why? Emmett would have to watch. After all, they were in a foreign country. It was easier for things to happen in a foreign country. They had no jurisdiction here, and although he'd reported being there, he had no backup.

Emmett followed Sabine and Donald out to the car, climbing into the back on his own. When he sat down, he could see Donald leaning across, his hand on Sabine's thigh. He hated the way she had to do this. Part of him wanted to turn round and chew the man out for treating a woman like this. But Sabine was good with it. She was playing her part. And she'd said to him before that she didn't mind doing that, for didn't Emmett have to play parts?

He sat back and looked down the road behind him. There were no cars there and as they drove off, nobody seemed to follow them. It was time to let the next part of this charade play out.

Chapter 10

The car felt warm as they drove along, and Emmett watched as Mackey's head lolled left and right as Sabine took corners. If he was acting drunk, he was certainly giving a good impression of it. He pointed down various roads, and soon they were heading out towards Alicante. Emmett followed their route with the maps function enabled on his phone, and soon they reached a cemetery.

It was miles away from Denia and Mackey's apartment, but Mackey was absolutely definite in where they were going. The sun was shining as Sabine parked up. Now out of the car, Emmett could feel a scorching sun. He was used to temperatures in the tens, but this felt close to twenties.

It was still not even fully spring and he wasn't sure if he could stick this heat full time. In his t-shirt and jeans, he watched as Sabine helped Mackey out of the car. He thought this was more so the man would feel her touch him once again and Mackey took her by the hand, walking along with her, saying he needed some support.

The cemetery was expansive, and they walked out to the far corner of it. This section was on the side of a hill, the path roughly cut in, but it flattened out to one side. In truth,

Emmett thought it wasn't an awful place to be buried. Not that anybody here would actually know.

The area had old headstones in it, but Emmett quickly spotted one that would have been from the last ten years.

'It's an old plot here,' said Mackey. 'That's where he is.'

He stood as Sabine and Emmett walked up close to the headstone. 'Carlos Hernandez' was the legend on the headstone. But at the bottom of the headstone, in italics, was the word 'Orca.' There was a small engraving of several islands and Emmett recognised them as the Orkneys.

'Obvious, isn't it?' said Emmett.

'That's what he asked for. Wanted to be remembered as coming from Orkney but, well, we couldn't put his name on it, could we? Couldn't have him buried under his real name. Would have raised questions back home.'

'Did he pay you much for this?' asked Sabine.

'Paid me enough. Living off of it.'

'How do you live?' asked Emmett. 'You certainly drink plenty.'

'I run a few favours for people here and there. Do some courier.'

'Not much of a life though, is it? You like the ladies, though.'

Mackey shot him a look. He turned and spoke to Sabine. 'I've been helpful to you. This is Orca. This is where he's buried. He died about ten years ago.'

'Any records?' asked Sabine.

'Carlos Hernandez is buried there. That's what you'll find. That's what it will say. Do I get anything from my help?' asked Mackey.

'Your help?'

'I'm a police informant,' said Mackey suddenly. 'You know,

77

I'm kind of like used to getting paid.'

Emmett shook his head, but Sabine stepped forward and placed a kiss on Mackey's cheek. 'You get my thanks,' she said. 'Might need to come back again.'

'You can come any time. Don't bring him,' said Donald.

'I'll take him back to the car,' said Sabine.

Emmett nodded, advising he'd be there in a few minutes. He stood beside the headstone, looking around. It was a grave that hadn't been opened at the same time as the rest. Why? Emmett wondered if there was even a grave under there. *They could have just put the headstone in. Authorities would have noticed, wouldn't they? It was a municipal graveyard. Used by lots of people. Nothing fancy. But then again, a perfect place to hide.*

Too easy, though, thought Emmett. *Why didn't Harlow just say the man was moved away, especially if he was now dead? Was the legend better to keep? Isbister was a dirty cop that killed himself. A sweet story that wraps everything up. Or did it? If you didn't have the destruction of McIntosh's firm beside it, it could work.*

A cop that got above his station. McIntosh was taken out and not by a rival. His men weren't arrested to languish in jail. They were killed. His organisation was taken down. No wonder Macleod was suspicious. Macleod was never put on any of it. Never tasked with those murders.

Emmett turned and walked back to the car where Mackey was chatting to Sabine in the front. He was telling her about a lifestyle that he'd lived, how he'd worked with top criminals, and how they were so reliant on him. Emmett found it amazing that a man would try to impress a female officer talking about criminals. After all, Sabine was the one who wanted to put them away.

Emmett sat in the rear seat in silence as Mackey continued

to talk to Sabine all the way back to his house. When they dropped him off, Sabine finally gave a sigh of relief.

'Man could talk for Britain,' she said. 'Loves himself too. Oh, he's gross when he touches you, though.'

'You didn't see his bedroom. He certainly likes the women,' said Emmett.

'I thought you all did. Well, nearly all of you.'

Emmett didn't take the bait, but continued to look out the window. 'Let's get somewhere to stay,' he said, 'on the coast near the beach. Might as well enjoy ourselves while we're here.'

'Good idea,' said Sabine. 'Make it look like we're done and dusted and flying back tomorrow.'

'Exactly. But it's all too simple, isn't it? It's all too, well—I don't like it.'

They found a hotel on the coast and booked into two separate rooms. And as it was getting round towards evening, Sabine suggested they take a walk along the beach.

Emmett had agreed and met her in the front lobby of the hotel. She was dressed in a T-shirt and jeans. Her black denim contrasted with his blue jeans, and he noted she was wearing a t-shirt from one of the comic cons. Her hair was loose, and she looked like she was ready to enjoy an evening.

They stepped out of the hotel, walking through various streets until they reached the beach, which stretched for at least a mile. The tide was halfway out. Little white breakers formed off a gentle roll-in and there was barely any wind. The evening was pleasant, warm enough without being boiling, and they started to walk. Sabine stopped after a moment, took her shoes off—and socks—and carried them in one hand.

'You do the same too,' she said. 'This sand's lovely.' Emmett did as he was told, for he always followed Sabine's advice on matters like this. It wasn't natural to him. The sand was almost a little chilly, especially when your feet dug into it. But he walked along with her before they stopped and stared out to the sea.

'Do you know something? When I told you about Harlow talking to me in the station, she said something else to me.'

'What?' asked Emmett.

'She talked about us like we were an item. Accused me of sleeping with you.'

Emmett felt slightly twitchy. 'How did that make you feel?' he asked.

'It didn't bother me,' lied Sabine. 'I know the truth and she was trying to wind me up. But I wonder what people see when they look at us. You know?'

'How do you mean?'

'Well, we're always together outside of work, you know. I think nothing of it because, well, we were going to get digs together. Wouldn't do that if I thought people were talking about us.'

'Or maybe they're just confused. I mean, a man and a woman can be friends, can't they? Close friends,' said Emmett.

He turned and looked up into her face, and she was looking back. She was smiling, but she was worried behind it.

'We are just friends, aren't we?' said Sabine. 'I mean, I've just come all the way up from Glasgow to stay working with you. I've let you be in charge, whereas I was, well . . .'

'You were the one who was on the dominant side in the Arts team. You were looking after me,' said Emmett. 'You had all the knowledge. I'm aware of that.'

'But you wanted me on this team, didn't you?'

'I did,' said Emmett. 'Clarissa works with Patterson. And I

think she does that because she saved his life. She maybe thinks he does it because he owes her something. But he admires something in her. He's more reserved. She's dynamic. As much as he shrugs his shoulders at her, he actually likes what he sees. Obviously not in any physical way but as a person.'

'That's what I feel about you,' said Sabine. 'I like you. You know that. You're a friend. We get on well together. That's why I wanted to move in. I can't think of any girlfriends who I'd want to share a house with. I just thought as colleagues it might be good. After all, we do lots of things together.'

'I thought it best that we didn't,' said Emmett. 'I like you a lot. Maybe it would give a poor signal. But that wasn't why I did it.'

'It's not like we've got anything physical between us, is it?' said Sabine, looking down at him, quizzical eyes looking back up at her.

'No,' he said. He turned and looked out to sea, knowing he'd lied. Of course he liked her physically, but he liked her in many ways. He was afraid, though. It wasn't easy being Emmett. It wasn't easy being so independent.

It was great having a friend beside him. One who accepted him. One who didn't question everything he did in life. Why he was the way he was and who liked him for it.

She reached over with her hand and touched his. 'I'm glad we're friends,' said Sabine. She stopped for a moment. Something was wrong. Emmett could sense it.

'Don't look now,' she said. 'There's a Spanish-looking man. I think he's following us.'

'Let's walk,' said Emmett. 'See if he follows.' As he turned, he thought he'd had a lucky escape. The moment was getting too serious. He wandered along, and suddenly Sabine stopped.

She turned, threw her arms around, hugging him. She whispered in his ear, 'He's still looking, still watching us.'

Emmett pulled her in tight. 'Let's lead him on.' They turned and walked along the beach, and Emmett put his hand into Sabine's.

After they'd walked about half a mile along, they came off the beach, put their shoes back on, and walked back to the hotel. Emmett asked her to come into his room. When he closed the door behind him, he sat down on the bed, allowing Sabine to sit in the chair in the room.

'It's all too easy, isn't it?' he said.

'You think?' said Sabine.

'They think we're close. They think we're doing this to get away. I want them to think that. Think we think we've wrapped this up and we're going to go back to Macleod and say, 'Here you go.' They don't know us that well.'

'He obviously thinks you're quirky. A strange one.'

'Well, I am,' said Emmett, 'but Macleod chose me because I've got something that he's got. I see it in Clarissa and in Hope too. There's a tenacity. There's a restlessness until you get to the bottom of a case.'

He looked over and saw Sabine smile at him. 'You have that,' she said.

'We need to do some investigating here. But I think you should spend most of the evening in here with me,' he said. He stood up and walked over to her, gazing at her. I hope you're ready,' said Emmett. 'This could be the highlight of your life.'

She stared at him. Emmett put his hand on her shoulder and bent down. He looked into her eyes, but his left hand was slipping past her, reaching into the bag that was sitting beside his chair. He pulled out a box the size of a playing card and held it in front of her.

'Zombieland 5. I'm going to take you out tonight.'

Sabine laughed. 'You haven't got a hope.'

Emmett stood up, took the cards out of the box and started dealing hands.

Chapter 11

Emmett was up early the next morning and joined Sabine for breakfast. They were booked on a flight at around eleven o'clock to return to the UK. As they sat having their morning meal, Emmett chewed on a croissant while Sabine polished off a full continental breakfast. Emmett could never see the point of cheese that early in the morning, but Sabine ate heartily.

'You all packed?' asked Emmett.

'Oh, we only brought a bag, didn't we? I wasn't for packing games.'

'But you're glad I did,' said Emmett. Sabine smiled.

'It's kind of nice not having someone over the top, like Clarissa. You work better as your own boss,' Sabine said to him.

Emmett thought about this. 'I've always been like that, though. I don't work well with people. You're quite different. I don't know why.'

'I'm used to sitting back and following and ignoring, being ignored. When I worked with Clarissa—'

'Are you seriously saying I'm like Clarissa?'

'No,' said Sabine. 'Less tartan.' She laughed at him.

Emmett smiled. 'Finish up,' he said. 'Come on, we'll get going. I want to check something out when we go to the flight.'

'We're not getting on it, are we?'

'Of course not,' said Emmett. 'But we have to take the hire car back. And then we'll try to use public transport. It could take us most of the day, I think, to get back.'

Sabine looked up at him. 'You want to go to the graveyard, don't you?'

'Of course. Who doesn't? We need to find out if it's him in there.'

'If it's not, that would blow it all apart. We'd know it was a lie. We could prove it was a lie. Then we have to work out why they're lying. We'll probably exonerate Isbister.'

'Let's not think like that at first. Let's just think on what we know. What has definitely happened.'

It was another sunny day as Sabine drove the car back to the airport. They dropped it off and wandered through to check in for their flights. They only had hand baggage, so they checked in and went through security.

There was someone following them the entire way. Emmett had clocked him from the car. The man was there in departures but of course couldn't move through security.

They'd arrived early for the flight by a good hour and a half. After half an hour of waiting in departures, Emmett and Sabine went to the help desk. They advised they couldn't make the flight and would have to re-book on a different one. When they stepped back outside into the main concourse of the airport, they looked around but could see no one untoward.

'Right,' said Emmett, getting onto his phone. 'Public transport it is.'

It took most of the day to get back over to Alicante and to the graveyard. The last part of the trip was completed on a local bus, and they walked a good half a mile up to the cemetery. Once they'd arrived, Emmett decided he would engage the manager and went to a large building, which seemed to be the hub of the graveyard.

It was quite quiet at the graveyard, although there was a funeral taking place in a far-off section. There was a receptionist, and Emmett, who wasn't fluent in Spanish but able to get by, ingratiated himself. He was then taken through with Sabine into an office in the rear. A man came through and Emmett greeted him in Spanish, but the man said his English was much better.

'Thank you,' said Emmett. He produced his warrant card and placed it in front of the man. 'I may not look like it,' he said, 'but I am Acting Detective Inspector Emmett Grump and this is Detective Sergeant Sabine Ferguson from the British Police. We just want to ask some questions about a particular gravestone.'

The man nodded, carefully inspecting the warrant card. 'Of course,' he said. 'Do our authorities know you're here?'

Emmett produced a piece of paper and placed it in front of him.

'That's who we've liaised with. Please feel free to ring them and clarify who we are.' Looking at the warrant card and then back to the number, the man simply nodded before handing them back to Emmett.

'Unless you ask for something important or private details, I'm quite happy to answer your questions,' he said. The man was young, maybe in his thirties. He had a large moustache, which made Emmett think he looked older than he was. His brown hair was smoothed down and the shirt he wore was neatly ironed. Sitting across from him, Emmett must have looked strange in his jeans and t-shirt.

'Gravestone for Mr Hernandez on the far side of the cemetery,' said Emmett. 'Do you remember much about it?'

'Which part of the cemetery?' asked the man, turning to look at a plot map that was on the wall of his office. Emmett stood and pointed it out. 'I remember that one well,' he said.

'Why?' asked Emmett.

'It was unusual. They said they had to be in that part. There was a tiny plot that hadn't been used. In fact, those who had bought it were found to be deceased, and I had it returned to the graveyard. Because of that, we could accommodate their request.'

'And Mr Hernandez, he was placed in there?'

'His ashes were placed in there,' said the manager.

'The ashes? So, you don't know if it was a Mr Hernandez?' asked Sabine.

'Well, the ashes came from the crematorium and were placed in.'

'And the plot was purchased, it was dug, and the ashes were put in?'

'Who paid for it, if you don't mind me asking?' said Emmett.

'It's funny,' said the manager, 'because you are from Scotland, yes?'

Emmett nodded. 'She isn't.' He pointed at Sabine.

'I am part Austrian, part Northern Irish,' said Sabine. 'My accent is different.'

'Yes, but you,' he said, pointing at Emmett, 'you have the same type of accent. It was a Scotsman, and I hadn't seen him before. He paid for it. Rather he came into the office when payment was required. Paid cash. I remember that.'

'And then he came back on the day, did he?' asked Emmett.

'No, no. No, he said it wasn't for him. He was merely funding it. There would be a relative coming.'

'How does it work?' asked Sabine. 'I mean how do you legally cremate someone here?'

'Well, you need an authorisation for cremation. You need permits. I don't deal with this. I just deal with the plots. You might look at the crematorium records. Carlos Hernandez. That's who you would look for.'

'Would the crematorium know his final resting place?' asked Emmett.

'No. Relatives could take the ashes home and leave them on the shelf. Many people do. They like to have family around them.'

'Of course,' said Emmett. 'So, there's no connection between the crematorium and the last resting place?'

'No. None at all. We obviously have more detail and look for authorisation when people have the bodies buried. That's different. We're operating very similar then to the way the crematorium does.'

'That's interesting,' said Emmett. 'Thank you for your help. I'd appreciate it if you didn't tell anyone, except obviously your police, that we were here.'

'And if my police ask?' said the man.

'Please inform them. Not a problem.' Emmett stood and shook the hands of the manager, followed by Sabine. The pair stepped back outside into the sunshine.

'That's interesting, isn't it?' said Sabine.

'Very,' said Emmett. He picked up his phone, dialling a number.

'Who are you looking to speak to?' asked Sabine.

'One moment.'

'Hello? Where are you, then?' said a female voice on the speakerphone.

'Not in the country. Do you mind if I borrow Ross for a bit?'

'Not at all,' said Hope. 'Bit early to ask for help from other teams, though, isn't it?'

'I don't want to deal with Macleod on this. Not sure he's going to be too happy Ross is looking into it. I think he wanted to keep the complete case between Sabine and I.'

'Well, I won't ask any more, then,' said Hope. 'As long as there's nothing nefarious.'

'No, it's just Ross is good. I need him to look up some foreign databases and chase through some crematorium records. That's all. Shouldn't take him more than an hour or two.'

'We are fairly quiet at the moment,' said Hope. 'Contact him directly. You can tell him I said it's fine.'

Emmett closed the call and phoned Ross directly.

'Acting Detective Inspector,' said Ross, hearing Emmett's voice.

'It's Emmett,' he said. 'Acting Detective Inspector's a mouthful. Especially when I'm a sergeant.'

'How can I help you?' asked Ross.

'I've cleared it with Hope. I want you to look into crematorium records in the Alicante area. We're looking for a Carlos Hernandez buried at the graveyard here in Alicante. I'll send you through addresses and details as best I can. May have also been cremated as a Mr Orca or a Mr Isbister.'

'I'll do what I can,' said Ross. 'How deep do you want me to dig?'

'Public records only, freely available,' said Emmett, 'or

certainly anything that a normal council worker or the like over here in Spain could get hold of. Nothing too risky. Don't expose yourself as digging in the records, everything nice and above board. You shouldn't have to hack into anything, at least not in too big a way.'

'Very good,' said Ross, 'and I get you on your mobile?'

'Yes,' said Emmett, 'we'll await your response. How long do you think you'll need?'

'If it's there, and it's in black and white, absolutely I'll be able to find it. If not, I'll give you a ring and tell you it's not.'

'Very good,' said Emmett, 'and thanks very much.'

'We've got to start you off on a good foot, I believe,' said Ross, and closed the call.

'What now then?' asked Sabine.

'We haven't really got anywhere else to go over here, have we? Not until Ross comes back to us.'

'No, we don't.'

Emmett stared around. He couldn't see anybody untoward. 'Come on,' he said. 'We'll get the bus.'

Together, the pair of them made their way on the half-mile walk to get to the bus. Climbing on board, they headed into town and spotted a backpacker hotel. It was a modern one in which they had large rooms, like closed off cubicles. They contained a bed, some other basic items and an en suite. Emmett booked in and the pair of them jumped inside, closing the doors to the outside world.

'If anybody's following us, they'll think we've just nipped off for a quick afternoon together,' said Emmett.

'What do we do?' asked Sabine, looking at him.

'Well, after I kicked your arse last night, do you fancy a rematch?' He reached into his bag and pulled out a small box of cards. 'Again?'

Sabine smiled. 'I didn't get this sort of attention from Clarissa.'

'I should hope not,' said Emmett.

'But you better be quick,' said Sabine. 'I've heard Ross is fast on the keyboard.'

'Not as fast as I am on the card deck,' smiled Emmett. He leaned forward on his knees and started dealing cards onto the bed. As he did so, Sabine looked up at him.

'You think it was wise going to the graveyard like that, to talk to the manager? He could tell people.'

'He could do, but at the moment, we need to operate legitimately. It's one thing to shake a tail; it's another thing to operate without supervision in somebody else's country. Police know we're here. We're investigating something. We've asked perfectly sensible questions,' said Emmett. 'If people find out about us and there's no tail, we'll know there's something else going on here. Trust me, it's like we're waiting for a mistake. They lined us up with a story. They wanted us to walk away thinking Isbister was in the ground. Till I know he is and where he is, my mind's completely open on what happened to him.'

'Won't they know that about you, too?' asked Sabine.

'I'm keen, new in the job. I'm trying to do my best for Macleod. This isn't ridiculous, what we're doing. And we'll see what comes. At the end of the day, I'm quite happy to follow their lead and then go back and report differently to Macleod. Give our suspicions then and see if he wants to open up the case more.

'I've got a bad feeling,' said Emmett, 'that this could be deep. Very deep. But for the moment, we operate simply. Remember, there was a man with a gun in my room. You don't wield guns like that, searching for stuff. Not police officers. Not unless you've got something serious to cover up.'

He smiled and dealt more cards. He hoped he didn't have to wait too long. Part of him would be happier once he got back onto UK soil.

Chapter 12

Emmett lay back on the bed, staring at the rather bland ceiling inside the cube that was their room. Sabine was sitting with her legs crossed at the far end of the bed, checking her phone. Looking at the ceiling, Emmett was running through his head exactly what he had seen.

He was wondering just who was involved with all of this. Macleod had put him onto this case, and yet it seemed to be such a long time ago. Macleod was dogged, determined, but clearly thought he couldn't investigate it himself or he would have. Or had he put it behind him? Had something else activated his interest in it?

Emmett could buy that Macleod might not tell him everything so that Emmett would come at it with fresh eyes. But he had a feeling that more than one party was in play here. The fact they were tailed almost constantly didn't smack of a case that was old and not worth bothering about. After all, McIntosh's gang was long gone. What was the problem?

Was there a secret to protect? And who had to protect that secret? If Isbister had been a genuine detective, hadn't been on the take, and hadn't murdered Matthews, then there would have been a cover-up. The tale that he was never found, that he disappeared, but yet seemingly committed suicide, would be a good one.

Emmett had thought that Macleod was an excellent judge of character. He had seemed to be, from what Emmett knew of him. Clarissa, for all that she ranted and raved about Macleod and said he wasn't this or didn't do that for her, seemed to have complete trust in his deductive abilities. Sabine too. So, it seemed strange to Emmett that he hadn't investigated this case much earlier and found something out.

What was worrying Emmett was he could be putting himself in danger more than usual. He liked the idea of going on to the cold cases because it wasn't in that thick of the action charge around. It was more thoughtful. More laid back. Possibly more like himself. He had the pleasure of working with Sabine as well.

He glanced over at her at the end of the bed, where she was staring at her phone. Emmett didn't make friends easily. He was cordial. He had his gaming group. But outside of the gaming, he didn't really do a lot. He thought of his hobbies. His painting. The board games he played on his own. He was a more solitary figure than most.

He didn't dress cool. He wasn't interested in heavy social-ising, yet he was interested in Sabine. She seemed interested in him as well. They went out together, not dates or anything like that. They just enjoyed their time together. He'd taken her under his wing with the board games and role playing, and in truth, she'd taken to it well. He couldn't have thought of anyone else he'd rather have as his partner working these cases.

It was so much easier than having somebody like Clarissa around, champing at the bit, hurling off in this direction or that. Sabine was more considered. And yet, he realised she was a good foil for him, because he would listen to her. She could also handle herself in a fight, much more than Emmett ever could.

His mobile phone buzzed and Emmett picked it up, seeing it was a call from Ross.

'It's Emmett here. What have you found out?'

'Well, it hasn't been that easy to dig into,' said Ross. 'But I used nothing that was overly complicated. I got into the crematorium records and found a Mr Orca. He's got a death certificate signed by a Dr Alejandro Perez. I checked up, and I've got a last known address for him near Alicante. However, one interesting fact was he was struck off from Spain's doctor's register for malpractice. I can't get too many other details about it. But I have the story. I'm sending you the address. I guess that gives you somewhere to start.'

'The man at the crematorium said you had to have a death certificate for the body to be burned.'

'I guess so,' said Ross. 'If you need anything else, call me, okay?'

'Of course,' said Emmett, 'and thank you. I appreciate it.'

By the time he switched the phone off and closed down the call, Sabine was staring at him.

'Address?' she asked.

'Yep, we're back off into Alicante, but I think we go there by public transport, no taxis. Here, he's just texted it through. Let's plot our route to get there,' said Emmett.

A few hours later, Emmett and Sabine left the building, taking their bags with them. They hopped on a bus, connected with another, and then walked a half a mile until they came up to the address that Ross had given them. It was now late at night, which suited Emmett much better. Easier in the dark to look at the place.

Sabine took a walk which was effectively around the block to make sure no one else was watching the building. There was a light on inside, but Emmett could see no movement as he monitored the building until Sabine caught back up with him. The pair quietly jumped a fence and ran quickly across a scorched lawn. Back home, the lawns were all green and lush. Especially in winter, they were damp and wet. But here, the lawn had not been tended in the summer months. It still looked barren.

Carefully, Sabine made her way across the veranda at the front of the house, while Emmett watched from the corner. He saw her get up to the front door. She pulled back a fly screen and then pushed the front door open. She came back, giving him a look. Surely, they locked their doors in Spain at this time of night?

Emmett crouched down and slowly made his way to the front door, where Sabine was about to enter. She slipped in quietly, followed by Emmett, who closed the door behind him.

'I can't hear anything,' said Sabine.

Emmett shook his head. He couldn't either. He stopped for a moment, listening, taking in deep breaths.

They were inside somebody's house in a foreign land with no jurisdiction. But at least the door had been open. They could always say they were trying to find the owner. They didn't have to break in. Sabine crept forward and then pointed to Emmett. In the darkness of the hall ahead lay a young woman, motionless and judging from the blood, also dead.

Carefully, Sabine made her way down a corridor to see a door lying open into a room. There were lights on inside.

Emmett watched as she stepped in. And then her footsteps halted after a few moments.

As he arrived at her shoulder, he saw another dead body, this time a young male. Emmett's heart thumped. He hadn't expected this. So far, the case had been interesting, to say the least. They'd been tailed. They'd had someone pull a gun on them when they found an intruder searching Emmett's room. But these people were dead.

'What age was Perez?' asked Sabine.

'When Ross texted, he said the man was in his fifties.'

'Well, neither of our bodies lying here then. Shall we search the rest of the house?' asked Sabine.

'Quickly,' said Emmett. 'I really don't like this and touch nothing.'

'Of course not,' said Sabine, and quickly stole off through another door. There was no sound in the house at all, and the quiet of outside was only broken by animals or buzzing insects.

There were two floors in the house, and Sabine made her way upstairs, closely followed by Emmett. A large bedroom lay off to one side, and on entering, they saw a large double bed and a man's body spread across it.

Carefully, Emmett walked up and stopped, looking down at the figure in front of him. It wasn't obvious how the man had died. He just looked to have passed quietly, if not for the rather slapdash appearance. There was no bruising, there were no marks, there was no large gash, but he was dead. He certainly looked it, and there was no breath coming from his mouth.

Sabine went to take a pulse, but Emmett grabbed her hand. 'Don't,' he said. 'The man will be dead.'

'Why do you say that?'

'Because the other two are,' said Emmett. 'They've done the job, whoever it is. They've killed everyone in this house.'

'But why?' asked Sabine. 'Why kill them all?'

'Because Perez would have known something,' said Emmett. 'Something that we would have found out. Or thought we would need to find out. He'd be the evidence. If he had done something unusual, it would be evidence.'

'So, how would they know we were coming here? I mean, he's recently dead, isn't he? He looks as if he could still be warm.'

'Well, he hasn't lost all the colour,' said Emmett, 'so he's not dead that long. Maybe they knew we were coming.'

'How would they know?' whispered Sabine.

Emmett shook his head. Slowly, the pair made their way back downstairs, standing just inside the front door.

'Can you hear something?' asked Sabine.

Emmett nodded. In the distance, there were sirens. They sounded like police sirens. They weren't quite the same as home, but they gave out that din. It was the sound that said 'we're coming and you'd better sort yourselves out.'

'We might be in trouble here. They'll come in numbers and maybe surround this place.'

'How do we explain being here?' asked Sabine. 'Maybe we should make ourselves known? Maybe we should phone through our concerns?'

Emmett shook his head. 'We do that, with everyone arriving here, and we won't have a clue who did this and why. This is what they want. Whoever's trying to hush this up, whoever's trying to cover up whatever happened, they want us to get embroiled. They want other authorities to be involved, then we'll be sent packing tail between our legs.'

'So, what do we do?' asked Sabine.

'We go home,' said Emmett. 'We need to go home. The first thing we must do is to get out of here and go to ground. We don't want to make a run for the airport just right now. With the police coming, they could surround this place soon. We need to move.'

'Follow me,' said Sabine. 'Quickly!'

She stole out through the front door. There were flashes of light in the distance. Sabine ran across the parched lawn until she got to the perimeter surrounded by a fence. Emmett watched as Sabine put a hand down on the wire fence and quickly leapt over it. Emmett tried to join her, one hand going on the wire, legs going up. But his foot caught the wire, and he tumbled down the other side. Sabine had him picked up and on his feet before he knew it.

'Head off down the street,' said Emmett.

'No,' said Sabine, 'no, we don't. Over there, that house.'

'We need to get out of here,' said Emmett.

'No, we don't until we see where they're coming from. Trust me,' said Sabine, 'you're on my soil now. This is what I'm good at.'

She turned, ran across the road and onto the property opposite. The lights were dark in the house and carefully she took Emmett's hand and stole around the side of it. She sat down on the ground behind a vehicle, Emmett joining her. From underneath the car, she could see out to the house they'd been in.

Police cars pulled up, and they watched for the next ten minutes as more and more pulled up. There was chatter in Spanish, Sabine saying that they were reporting the deaths and that more units were on their way. Soon they would come calling around the different houses, asking if anyone had heard anything. There was a cordon of officers being set up around the house, fortunately over the other side of the road. Lying behind a car in the driveway, the pair were out of sight. Sabine tapped Emmett on the shoulder.

'Now we can go. The focus is all on the inside. Soon they'll start widening out and talking to neighbours. We need to be away from here by the time they get here. I suggest we don't use any public transport. Walk for about the next hour or two. Get well clear and then decide what we're going to do.'

Emmett gave her a nod and indicated she should lead the way. They tried to stay close as they cut this way and that, past some bushes round the back of a house and soon they were out walking along streets.

Alicante was fairly built up and people out at this time of the day were not that unusual. But Sabine didn't take a risk and kept to the back streets as best she could, out where places were not lit, where there were no streetlights. Slowly, she made her way back into the more built-up areas. After a while, they'd reached the edge of urban Alicante. Sabine stopped Emmett and turned to him.

'You've just witnessed three dead,' she said. 'We should report it to the authorities. Report who the people were, or at least who one of them was. Say what we're looking into.'

'Not at the moment,' said Emmett. 'I think we need to keep this going. We've just seen a massive attempt at covering up performed before us. One thing we must do, is to stay clear. Get home. Get back on our soil. I don't know over here who we can trust.

'By the looks of it, Dr Perez didn't know either. He's held a secret. And it must be to do with signing that form. He obviously knew something. Something that was now worth killing him for. And also trying to plant on us.'

'But we could go to the authorities,' said Sabine. 'That way we could be better protected and then fly back.'

'We're not sure back home who's involved. I have even less idea over here. I think it's wise that we give the authorities a wide berth. We did our duty in saying we were here. We don't want to sign our own death warrants.'

'Well, you're the boss,' said Sabine, 'and if that's the case, let's get going because I want to get home soon.'

Chapter 13

Emmett gave a sigh and turned his head slightly. As he did so, it connected with the shoulder of Sabine. He leant with his back to her, and somehow slipped down slightly on the seat, so when he turned, her shoulder dug into him. It caused her to rouse, and she sat up, giving herself a shake.

Emmett looked and saw that the jacket she'd put under her head had fallen down onto the seat, and he grabbed it, giving it back to her.

'You okay?'

'I didn't really get much sleep,' she said. 'You?'

'No. It won't be that long until our bus, though.'

It was half-past five in the morning, and the pair were sitting at the back of a bus station in Alicante. They were out of the way, but even so, Emmett couldn't settle. Nobody had seen them leave the house. Nobody had known where they'd gone. They'd wandered through the streets, keeping to the shadows, until they'd needed to find a bus. Emmett had discovered that the first one wasn't going until half-past five.

Emmett stood up and stretched, and then sat back down again. The bus station was fairly empty, only the occasional local walking about. Most of them were staff. There were a few other tourists sleeping. They looked like they were young backpackers. Sabine and Emmett didn't cut that image. Maybe ten years to twenty years too old.

At five in the morning in Spain, it was still chilly—although it had nothing on a good Scottish morning. Scottish mornings, you could get up and try to see if the hospital would transplant a duvet onto you, such was the chill. Here it was just a change of temperature. He wasn't truly cold. His brain was just telling him it wasn't as warm as it had been.

There were a few people wandering about the bus station. Some drunks. People who had been lost the night before. And there were a few people who also worked there. One or two were behind large grills, waiting until the hour when they would open up and sell tickets.

'How did they know you were going there? We had absolutely nothing until Ross called that in,' said Emmett.

'I need Ross to check. I think they've found out. Found out what he told us. Spotted him digging here, there, and wherever. It was almost too easy for him.'

'You think Perez was a plant?' asked Sabine.

'Not a plant. Dr Perez was dead. I think what they wanted was to trap us. Have a major incident. Macleod couldn't continue to run the investigation then. If he was instructed to close it off, it would be harder for him to keep going with this. Someone got on to us. Somebody saw what Ross was doing,' said Emmett. He picked up his mobile phone and dialled Ross's number.

'What is it?' said a voice as the call was answered.

'Did you, by any chance, get clocked checking up on Dr Perez for us?' asked Emmett.

103

'Hang on,' said Ross. 'Give me a moment.'

Emmett could hear Ross asking someone if it was okay, and then Ross moving across his room. Emmett could hear the keys being tapped on the keyboard. But he waited in silence, aware that Ross was doing his job.

'Possibly. But it's someone clever. Someone cleverer than me,' said Ross. 'And I'm no dummy with these things.'

'Are they able to track us?' asked Emmett.

'What do you mean?' asked Ross.

'You investigated. We went to the address you'd given. Now, somebody must have been aware you were looking at Dr Perez, or they've intercepted a message from us.'

'Are they're tailing you? Have you seen them?'

'No, there was literally no one about. But when we got to Perez's house, he was dead.'

'I'm not sure how they've tapped into me. Somebody's doing it back here. I think you should get home,' said Ross.

'I'm trying to,' said Emmett. 'I'll call Macleod.'

He closed the call and Sabine looked over at him. 'Problems?'

'Ross thinks he may have been traced in what he was doing. I mean, that may have been why they knew we were going there, which meant that Perez was a key factor. He must have done something, something that would show up. Something that would tell us. Something definite about who was in that grave.'

'Do we stick around then? Try to find out more?'

'My instinct is no. I don't know how big this is,' said Emmett. 'I'm going to phone Macleod.'

The phone rang eight times before there was a muffled voice that said, 'Macleod, what's the crisis?'

'Good morning, Detective Chief Inspector,' said Emmett. 'I

have to inform you we've been looking into a Dr Perez who signed the death certificate of a Mr Orca. Dr Perez signed the death certificate for the man we believe to be Isbister, who then got buried in a graveyard in Alicante. However, Dr Perez is dead. We went to his house, and there were three bodies.'

'What do you mean, "There were three bodies"?' blurted Macleod.

'Front door was open. We went in, and we found three bodies. Dr Perez, a young man, and a young woman. There isn't a mark on any of them, as far as I can tell.'

'You didn't touch them, did you?'

'No,' said Emmett. 'I'm not daft.'

'So where are you?'

'I'd rather not say over the phone.'

'I got a call last night late, eleven o'clock, from upstairs. I had to go in, and they came down to my office. People are asking questions about what you're doing. Proper questions.'

'That's a good thing, isn't it?' said Emmett. 'That's what we want. We know we're on the right track then.'

'That's one way of putting it,' said Macleod. 'But when people that high up start asking questions at eleven o'clock at night, and not simply just call you in the morning, it means somebody higher up has got hold of them. You weren't doing anything untoward. Also warned the police you were out there. You visited a graveyard? Have you been tailed?'

'We've been keeping an eye, but there have been moments.'

'I need to contact someone,' said Macleod. 'Don't move from what you're doing. I'll get back to you in a couple of minutes.'

Emmett closed the call and saw Sabine smile at him. 'What's the big boss say?'

'Big boss got a visit from even bigger bosses,' said Emmett.

'Seems somebody doesn't like us being here.'

'What's Macleod suggesting?' asked Sabine.

'Nothing yet. He's gone off to contact someone. I'm not sure who.'

'I bet he's trying to find out if there's secret service involvement,' suggested Sabine.

'Possibly, I guess,' said Emmett. 'But this all seems strange. Carried out over here. If the man was committing suicide and you wanted rid of him, you'd just do it over there. Bury the body, weigh it down in the ocean. Something like that. Why would you come all the way over here and have a facade that said he was buried here? Why would you even leave a trace to him? We were directed here, remember. We didn't get our way to here. The initial pointer came from Harlow.'

'How did Harlow know what we were doing? Very helpful. Very.'

'Too helpful,' said Emmett. 'Being pointed, being directed.'

The phone rang again, and Macleod was on the other end.

'I've just spoken to someone in the know. She doesn't believe this is secret service. That means there're parties at work here that are not the normal parties. Get home. Get back to the UK as quick as you can. Don't look into anything else. Stay quiet and get home.'

'I was planning on it,' said Emmett. 'Hopefully, I'll see you today.'

He closed down the call and looked over at Sabine. 'I think we're digging up a bigger hornet's nest than we realise. He wants us home, now!. That means he doesn't think we're safe.'

'Well, I was kind of getting the feeling,' said Sabine. 'The bus should be here in another ten minutes.'

They sat there for another five minutes before Sabine went

up and bought a couple of tickets for the bus due to leave five minutes later. They made their way over to the stand, but the bus hadn't yet arrived, and there were a few other people queued up. It wasn't, however, busy. But it was still dark, and a little light rain was falling. It wasn't bothering Emmett as he still felt warm; it wasn't like a cold Inverness drizzle.

'That'll be our bus over there,' said Sabine.

Emmett looked up and saw in the distance one rolling over towards the station. It would follow the road down towards their stop if all went well. Meanwhile, Sabine was checking her bag, putting it over her shoulder, and Emmett lifted his, too.

And then Emmett saw him walking towards them. The man wore a large-brimmed hat. He had jeans on, as well as a long jacket. The man wouldn't look Emmett in the eye, looking everywhere else as he walked along. Emmett knew that the man was walking with a purpose. He glanced back occasionally, looking towards the bus. Emmett nudged Sabine.

'The man coming towards us,' he said.

'Old guy, maybe sixty, heavy tan,' said Sabine.

'That's the one. He keeps looking at the bus and not looking directly at us. Looking over towards us, to either side of us. But he's walking directly for us. You always look for some points to where you're going.'

'You think he's a—'

'A what?' said Emmett. 'A spy? A hitman? I don't know. I'd also feel better moving at the moment because he could be just somebody walking along.'

The bus was getting closer now, and in front of it were several cars. The man continued looking back.

'Do we move? Get out of here?'

'No,' said Emmett. 'We wait. If he gets really close, however, be prepared in case he pulls a knife.'

The man had walked quicker and kept glancing back to where the bus was getting closer and closer. It was going to outpace him to Emmett, and Emmett wasn't surprised when the man burst into a run. The long jacket flailed out behind him, but as the man got closer, he didn't glance back at the bus. He glanced at a car ahead of the bus.

Emmett was observing the man, bracing himself, ready to take him on. But then he saw the window of the car behind him. It was rolling down. The man was now less than ten feet away, accelerating rapidly. But so was the car.

Something was shouted in Spanish, and the man flung himself forward, catching Emmett in the midriff. He took Emmett down to the ground in what would have been called an excellent rugby tackle. Beside him, Sabine hit the deck as quickly as she could. The car raced past, almost crashing and without stopping. Emmett was almost panicking now, lying on the ground. He went to push the man off, but the man held him down briefly before getting up on his knees.

'You go,' he blurted. 'You go.'

'Where? Why?' said Emmett. 'I have a bus to catch.'

'Emmett,' said Sabine, and she was pointing to the wall behind him. Emmett looked and saw two holes; bullet holes. It must have been a silenced weapon. The man reached and grabbed Emmett's hand, pulling him up to his feet. He waved at Sabine, and Emmett saw a car up ahead, turning round again. The man took them into the bus station.

'We should head off in our own direction,' said Sabine, shouting after Emmett.

'No, with me, with me,' said the man.

He ran down a flight of stairs, Emmett staying close on his tail.

'We keep going,' said Emmett, 'we keep going.'

Down, down they went, causing people to turn and stare. The bus station wasn't busy, but it was reasonably large.

It was two minutes before they emerged back out onto the street. It was at the rear of the station and sweeping in off the street was a taxi rank. The man ran along it, not taking the first taxi on the rank, but going to one five down.

'David,' the man said, and then uttered something in Spanish. Emmett looked back at Sabine.

'Airport. He wants us to go to the airport.'

'In,' said Emmett, 'in.' The man who had led them had opened the door and practically shoved Emmett anyway, as well as Sabine, before closing the door and running off. David, who presumably was the driver, then indicated and drove out, speeding away into the early morning.

Emmett sat back, staring at the driver in front, then looking around. He reached down to his phone and drew up the map, looking for where the airport was.

'Are we going the right way?' asked Sabine.

'You go the right way,' said David in the front. 'I will take you. You stay low, you get on a plane, you get out of here. Get through security. Once through security, you'll be safer. Not on the main concourse.'

Emmett gave a nod and looked over at Sabine. He saw her tremble. He could feel his own hands beginning to shake. It had been half five in the morning and if it hadn't been for that man chasing them, and knocking him to the ground, he'd probably be dead.

Emmett was sweating by the time they reached the airport.

He was trying desperately to keep himself from thinking bad thoughts, only about the actions he needed to take. Stepping out of the taxi, they quickly went through and bought a ticket on the first flight out. It wouldn't take them to Scotland. It would take them straight into London, but it was departing in forty minutes. They would have just enough time.

They made straight away for security, passing through it and then standing on the other side. Emmett made sure they stayed near crowds without going too far into them. Fifteen minutes later, they were making their way onto the plane.

Sitting down in the plane, they noted two seats either side of the aisle. Sabine was sat on the inside of a pair, Emmett nearest the window of the same pair. She'd insisted, for she was the better fighter. She was the one who could handle herself if someone came—not Emmett.

They sat there, then watched as the safety demonstration was given, and the plane taxied out. With the wheels up, and their ears beginning to feel the pressure of climbing, they both breathed a sigh of relief.

Sabine reached over and put her hand in Emmett's. It was sweaty, and she clutched his hand. She turned to look at him, and Emmett could see tears coming down her face.

'They missed,' said Emmett, but his own heart was thumping, his mind going back to the bus stop. He couldn't put it out of his head.

Sabine looked at him. 'They missed. Good job. Good bloody job,' she said. She leaned over, her head going on Emmett's shoulder, and he slipped an arm round and pulled her close. He'd almost lost his friend today. She'd almost lost him. She lay with her head on his shoulder for most of the flight.

And his hands couldn't stop sweating.

Chapter 14

E mmett wasn't happy simply returning to Inverness. The case had begun at Pitlochry and involved the Glasgow murder team. So rather than race all the way home, he thought he should do more snooping in that general area. However, he knew also that he didn't want to do things too fast. After their plane arrived in Glasgow, Emmett booked Sabine and himself into a small hotel on the outskirts of Glasgow.

He called Macleod, asking to meet up the next day. Macleod advised he would bring Ross with him, as Ross had reported the work he'd done for Emmett. The call was quick, functional, and Emmett wondered if Macleod had difficulties dealing with him.

Emmett was aware he was the only male detective inspector amongst Macleod's departments. He had seen him work with Clarissa and, while she was fiery, he challenged her. He would constantly jab at her and bring out the best of her. Hope McGrath was different, and he saw how Macleod brought out her standards, complementing Macleod.

A man who had a wingman in Hope and a Rottweiler in Clarissa. Emmett wondered what he was to Macleod. Just the right person in the right place or was he someone to be not used—for that was too strong a word—but someone whose talents were to be brought out?

Sabine drove Emmett to the services on the north side of Glasgow. Once there, they made their way through to the cafe, sitting down in the corner with a sandwich and a coffee. Approximately twenty minutes later, Macleod walked in with Ross at his heels. Emmett watched as Macleod strolled over, turned to give Ross an order for coffee, and then sat down in the seat opposite.

'Safe,' said Macleod. 'That's good to see.'

'Shall we wait for Ross?' said Emmett. 'I want to know about whether he was hacked or followed when he went on the computers.'

'I think he's got information on that,' said Macleod, and simply nodded. It was quiet then, neither Macleod nor Emmett saying anything, until Sabine pitched in.

'Getting quite strung out, this case, isn't it?'

'So far,' said Macleod and stayed quiet again.

'A little more action than I thought we were going to get,' said Sabine.

Emmett said nothing, simply waiting until Ross returned with two coffees, and sat down.

'If I may,' said Emmett to Macleod, and then turned to Ross. 'Did you find anything out about whether you'd been traced when you were looking up information for me?'

Ross almost went red. 'I think I was, but I was hacked internally,' he said.

'Internally?'

Macleod turned and looked at him.

'I think it's come from within, but possibly a Glasgow

terminal,' said Ross. 'I need to do a bit more work on it. There's a programme running at the moment. I should know soon.'

'Good,' said Emmett, and then sat there.

The silence was deafening, and Sabine took up the reins just to fill the space that had been left behind.

'It really was tight out there,' she said, and detailed to Macleod everything that had happened. Occasionally, she would glance at Emmett, but he said nothing. He simply sat there, staring into his coffee. Macleod, however, engaged freely with Sabine, nodding his head and occasionally furrowing his brow.

'And you say they just shot at you, but the silencer—'

'Exactly,' said Sabine. 'If it hadn't had been for that man, we'd have been dead. I don't mind saying it. It's not what I signed up for. It's not spy work I'm in. This was meant to be a cold case. I thought there'd be lots of forensics, lots of digging up the past. Not hiding out in a foreign country.'

'Do you think Isbister's buried out there? Do you think that was his grave?' asked Macleod. For a moment, Sabine looked at Emmett, but he was still staring deep into his coffee.

'I don't know. The doctor fudged the records or did something with them. And he's dead because of it. It's going to be difficult to get any clarity. If anyone is in that loop and knows he's dead, knows that somebody killed him, well, why would you speak? We are definitely on to something.'

'Could be a double bluff,' said Macleod.

'It's a lot to kill somebody for a bluff,' said Sabine.

'Not necessarily,' said Macleod. 'What else did you find?'

Sabine went to speak, but Emmett suddenly put his hand in front of her and looked up at Macleod.

'Why is this here?' said Emmett suddenly. 'Why is this case

in front of us? Why are we investigating this? It's not a cold case. It's a missing person believed deceased. Someone they believed took their own life. Now suddenly, we're running across Europe, looking for someone's grave. Being directed in. We're being followed. I had my stuff searched. We're shot at. We're then saved by a strange party.'

'I couldn't look at it myself,' said Macleod. 'At the time, I was pushed onto other things. Now, well, I've got distance between it. I wanted fresh eyes on it. I wanted somebody else to take a look.'

'Liar,' said Emmett. He watched Macleod's face. He expected it to become angry. But instead, the man sat there passively.

'Why do you say that?' asked Macleod.

'Because it's not true,' said Emmett. 'If you'd wanted this looked at for all those years, you'd have had Hope onto it. You've got Perry. He thinks like you. That's what they say. You've had Clarissa if you wanted the dust kicked up. But no, no, you don't do anything. You open up a cold case branch. I know you were pushing for that. It was part of what you wanted to do up in Inverness. And the first thing you do is hand us a case that's not a cold case. Something completely different. Why?' asked Emmett.

'I said I wanted fresh eyes on it,' said Macleod, now slightly more tense.

'No, you had Hope, Hope McGrath, by-the-book Hope McGrath; Hope McGrath, who would make sure that all the I's are dotted and the T's are crossed. She could work in the face of everyone else and say this is a justifiable case, and they couldn't come after her on it. Or did you not want to put her in the line of fire? Is that it? Are we expendable?'

'That's not correct,' said Macleod.

'So what? Why me? I'm an unknown quantity. Suddenly throw me up to DI. Why am I on this case? Why is Sabine on this case?'

'Sabine's on this case because you want her with you,' said Macleod. 'She's the one person who you work well with. Don't get me wrong, you're a good detective, but you're insular. You don't work well with other people. Not overly. They see you as strange. It's not all your fault. In fact, most of it isn't your fault. People need something. Even from me, they need that rapport. As I've seen, Sabine and you work well together. You asked for her to be on the team. Seems sensible to me. That's why she's here.'

'And I'm here because?' asked Emmett.

'Because you think differently. You can spot things. You're not the same as Perry. He's very good, and he does think like me, but you don't think like me,' said Macleod. 'You think differently. You look with no ego, you look with no agenda, and you see people slightly differently than I do. That's why I wanted you.'

'Rubbish, absolute rubbish. Don't you get it? I can see that, I can see through it. You made a decision at some point that you were not investigating this matter. You had reconciled yourself to it. It may have been difficult to live with, it may have been something you had to think about, you may have woken up at nights and thought 'can I leave that?' But you did. You're Macleod. You're known for being who you are, known for being the way you are. Thorough. So, if you could get into this, if you could dig it up, you'd do it. But you decided to leave it.'

'Waiting the right time,' said Macleod.

'No, you weren't. You level with me or I'm out that door,'

said Emmett. 'I am out that door and I won't come back.'

Macleod leaned forward and took a sip of his coffee. When he placed the cup back down, he reached inside his jacket, pulled out an envelope, and threw it down in front of Emmett.

'Arrived the day before you walked into your office for the first time,' he said. 'Read it.'

Beside him, Ross was agape. Sabine was also sitting with her mouth half open. Emmett thought they were about to collapse.

Emmett opened up the letter and looked at the simple words written inside. *'Poor Isbister,'* he hissed. *'How did you finish him? So what? Is it guilt?'*

'No,' said Macleod. 'Somebody knew how to get at me. I'm not someone to walk away, but back then I was younger. And Isbister? I couldn't be sure. Didn't think he was dodgy, but then there was the note. I'm not that good with suicide. People close to me have, well . . . gone that way. I was taken away as well, not allowed onto cases. Meanwhile, the whole of McIntosh's firm went down, and I was glad to see the back of them. The stuff they'd done, people they'd killed. It was good for them to be out of the way.

'And I live with that,' said Macleod. 'I'm different now. Somebody banked on it, and they calculated correctly.'

Emmett looked back at the letter before folding it up and handing it to Macleod. 'I take it there was—'

Macleod shook his head. 'Nothing on it. No fingerprints except for the postman's.'

'What's going on?' asked Sabine. 'Where's that come from?'

Emmett sat back for a moment and then shook his head. 'Our dear DCI has dropped us right in it, Sabine.'

'What do you mean?' she asked.

'Somebody wants him to look into this case because something's wrong. Isbister didn't commit suicide, didn't do what they said he did. But somebody else is portraying a story the other way. And because Isbister worked for the police, it's somebody on the inside. It's somebody connected with the police. And possibly the very people that DCI Macleod here worked with.'

'I couldn't very well walk in myself. I'm kind of known,' said Macleod. 'But you? You're different. Sabine gets on with people. She's got a way. You're the opposite. People give you a wide berth, and they never know what you're thinking, where you're coming from. Never know what you'll do,' said Macleod.

Emmett put his fist on the table, gently, but it was clenched. 'You put us in jeopardy.'

'I didn't intend to. I still don't know how far this stretches—what it is,' said Macleod. 'I may have thought there might have been a cover-up. There may have been dodgy dealings, but not like this.'

'And we checked that it's not our friends in the Service?'

'I asked someone who used to work for them,' said Macleod. 'She said it's not them. It's definitely not them.'

Emmett blew out a large breath, again shaking his head. 'Which means that it's somebody else with influence. There's a dark figure at play. But there's also a dark figure prompting us into things. Somebody who knows. Knows the lie. But they can't expose it. Because if they could, they'd do it. Maybe they're not reputable enough. You're reputable enough,' Emmett said to Macleod. 'That's why they're wanting you to do it. Maybe because you were tied in. And they've played you, haven't they? They've played you because it's pricked your

117

conscience bad enough to throw us into this.'

'It has,' said Macleod. 'But if you want, you can walk away. I'll go in myself. I'll look at it.'

'No,' said Emmett suddenly. And then he turned to Sabine. 'If it's okay with you.'

'Where you go, I go,' said Sabine.

Emmett turned back to Macleod. 'Somebody shot at me. Somebody tried to kill me. I want to know who that was. Don't take kindly to it. I especially don't take kindly to someone wanting to kill my friend.'

There was a quiet resolve around the table. And then Ross's phone cut through the silence with an audible bing.

Chapter 15

'Just give me a minute,' said Ross, and pulled his phone out onto the table. There was an awkward silence as he looked. Emmett stared at Macleod. A minute later, Ross turned back to them.

'You were stationed down in Glasgow. You were there recently, weren't you?' said Ross.

'Yes,' said Emmett. 'Well, I wasn't. But Sabine went in.'

'That's where Harlow spoke to me,' said Sabine. 'That's where we got the lead to go to Spain.'

'Well, I was hacked from a terminal in there,' said Ross. 'At least that's what I believe. I'm having difficulty pinning it down as to which one it would be.'

'Is there any way we can assist with that?' asked Emmett.

'Not sure,' said Ross. 'Maybe. Give me a minute.' He stood up and walked out of the cafe, leaving Macleod, Emmett, and Sabine waiting at the table.

'What are you thinking?' asked Macleod.

'I don't do well,' said Emmett, 'being played about. We need to go after them, whoever's doing this. They've sold us a version of the truth. Harlow deliberately sent us to Spain. I think they want us to believe that your friend is lying in a grave out there. Make it out that he was clever enough to get himself clear, lived out his life, and then was buried. And then everyone will leave everything alone.'

'What bothers me,' said Macleod, 'is why it's so important—the truth about Isbister. Nobody's going to get overexcited that the McIntoshes are gone.'

'That's true. Most of you involved must be quite old now,' said Sabine.

'Exactly,' said Macleod, 'but even if somebody did something to Orca, the problem is proving it after all these years. And also what to do about it. It won't come to us easy. It'll be a long, hard fight. There'll be a slog through the courts trying to prove anything.'

'Also, remember that we're being pushed into this. Couldn't be his wife, could it?' asked Emmett.

'No. She remarried. Moved on. Fairly quickly as well,' said Macleod. 'Although I never knew her that well.'

'When you say not well. Did she know you at all?'

'Never been round to the house. I knew of her. I knew what Isbister said about her. That was it. He didn't talk to me about wives because he knew my background and how I'd lost mine up in Stornoway. Few people talk to me about their happy families knowing how I had lost mine. More about cases.'

'And outside of this case, outside of looking into the murder at Pitlochry, was there any other cases that were bothering you?' asked Emmett.

'I hadn't worked with him that long to do many. In fact, we hadn't done any at all,' said Macleod.

'So it's somebody else. Somebody has come to you. Maybe because of your fame.' Macleod looked at him. 'No. Your fame. You're known. Like Hope. I'm not. Clarissa's not.'

'She is getting a name for herself,' said Macleod.

'But maybe somebody's looking for justice, in that sense,' said Emmett. 'Maybe they're pushing you in that sense. They just know. Or maybe they think you were more involved than you were. But somebody is covering up.'

Ross arrived back. 'I think it was a laptop plugged into the terminal. Do you want me to go after this?'

'We need to be careful,' said Macleod. 'If they've come with a gun, and they were going to eliminate Sabine and you,' Macleod said to Emmett, 'then they'll surely come after us if we disturb other things.'

'More difficult to do though,' said Emmett. 'Worth the risk. We need to be careful with it. Clever.'

'I could,' said Ross, 'get you a small device that you can plug into the laptop. You should be able to find if it was on the terminal.'

'But how do we go for the laptop?' said Emmett.

'We pick who we think it is,' said Sabine. 'Harlow works there. Let's go and try Harlow's. We're coming fast at this and yet we haven't asked the question. Are we looking into a grand scale cover-up or just one or two people?'

'Grand scale,' said Macleod. 'It's got to be. They've tried to kill you in a foreign land. Tailed you over there. That takes some organisation.'

'But the cover-up within the station could be very simple and could be one person. With wider links,' said Emmett. 'Sabine's right. We try Harlow.'

'So you've got to get in there and get whatever device Ross has given you onto her laptop. That will not be easy. I mean, who are you asking to do that?' mused Macleod.

'Leave that up to us. You take yourself back up the road, sir,' said Emmett. 'Your being about will not help. If you're here, they'll think we're on to something big. They'll think we're getting very close. More likely to do more harm to us. Better if you aren't here. Keep it small. Sabine and me. No one else. We can also disappear easier that way.'

'Okay. But be careful,' said Macleod. 'And if it gets too much, walk away.'

'I walk away, and you'll walk in,' said Emmett. 'Best chance we've got is me going on with this.'

'Well, good luck then,' said Macleod. 'Keep me informed.' He stood up, and nodded to Ross. Ross said he would be just a moment, and Macleod left the cafe.

'I don't believe you called him out like that,' said Sabine.

Emmett turned over to look at Ross. 'You ever know him to lie like that?'

'No,' said Ross. 'He's kept it from you for a reason. He may have wanted genuinely fresh eyes. Or a way for you to walk back out.'

'What have you got for me?' asked Emmett.

Ross reached down into his coat pocket. He pulled out a small device and placed it on the table.

'Put it into the USB connection. Make sure the laptop's on. All you've got to do then is leave it in place. It'll probably take about two, three minutes to do it. I can't tell exactly. But when it's done, the little light on the side here will go out. It'll go on as soon as you put it in.'

'Simple as that?' said Sabine.

'Simple as that. And then send it to me.'

After having a bite of lunch, Emmett and Sabine headed to the station that they used to occupy. Sabine warned Emmett about the reaction they might get when they walked in.

Emmett wasn't bothered. Nobody ever paid him good attention. Well, except for Sabine and his friends at the gaming. He was a geek; he was strange, and it didn't bother him. They parked the car and came in via the rear entrance. As soon as they did so, Emmett could sense the hostile atmosphere.

'I'll create the diversion,' said Sabine. 'Be ready to go for it.'

Emmett followed Sabine down the corridors until they came to the offices of the murder unit in the station. A rather noisy office became incredibly quiet as Sabine walked in, Emmett lingering a short distance behind. Through an inner office window on the far side, Emmett could see DCI Harlow working. She had a large desktop computer and Emmett couldn't see a laptop. He held back, out of sight of the main office and Harlow's own space.

'Good afternoon,' said Sabine. 'Detective Sergeant Sabine Ferguson, but you all know me, anyway. You probably know why I'm here. I need to get some details on a former case and trace some officers that used to be in this unit.'

'Got a bit of nerve coming all the way down from there,' said a voice.

Sabine recognised the man. She didn't like him. Not one bit. He'd looked down on the Art unit when she was in it. *Not proper policing.* But she also thought he had small man syndrome. She stood at least five inches taller than he. And he was one of those people who belittled you while checking you out at the same time. DC Hagen was a relic before his time.

'You'll do,' said Sabine, walking over to the man. 'I've got a list here. A case that was up in Pitlochry. Death of Ian Cullen. I think Harlow was one of the team.'

'DCI Harlow,' said Hagen. He was bald and rotund, but he could spit fire.

123

'She wasn't the DCI then, though, was she? I need the details. I need the other officers who were there. Those that were retired. I'm going to need to conduct some interviews.'

'You can't just barge in here like this,' said Hagen. 'It's not proper protocol. You're not in the Art team now.'

Sabine strode over, towering over the man. Her six-foot height and long black hair now falling down in front of her, almost touching the top of his head as he sat in his seat.

'I don't care. I need help and I need it now. My DI wants this stuff and we're going to get it. Frankly, you need to cooperate.'

'I don't need to do anything,' raged Hagen. Sabine reached over to where a pile of what looked like paperwork sat on the desk. With her left hand, she flicked it, sending it to the floor.

'What the bloody hell are you doing?'

'Getting you off your arse,' said Sabine.

Hagen was up and out of his seat, pushing himself forward against her, but Sabine stood her ground.

'You don't have to take that crap,' said one of the other officers. And then she heard the voice she wanted to hear.

'What's going on here?'

There was a sudden silence in the room and out walked DCI Harlow into the main office.

'I require a little assistance,' said Sabine.

Emmett had hung back, almost round the corner, watching DCI Harlow walk over. All eyes were on her. He crouched down, crawling behind desks, as Sabine continued her charade. Entering Harlow's office, Emmett could see a laptop bag. He reached over and grabbed it before taking the laptop out, and placing it on the floor of the office.

'Shall we go into my office and discuss this? Where's your detective inspector? Have you not brought him with you?'

thundered Harlow.

'Oh, he's looking at other things,' said Sabine.

'You were offered assistance!'

'You call that assistance? That wasn't assistance. That was a wild goose chase. Are you covering something up?' said Sabine.

Emmett didn't look up. He was crouched down in Harlow's office. He opened up the laptop and jabbed the device with the USB connection into the side of the laptop.

There was a screen for a password, but Emmett touched nothing. He watched as the device emitted a little red light. It needed to be quick. Really quick.

'If you're not careful, I'm going to get someone up here to escort you out, Detective Sergeant,' said Harlow suddenly. 'I might need to talk to your boss.'

'The DI is out and about conducting further investigations,' said Sabine.

'I'm talking about Macleod. He wouldn't appreciate this behaviour.'

'He wouldn't appreciate things being hidden. Have you had people following us?'

'What's that meant to mean?'

'Are any of these juniors involved with you? Or is it just you?' *Juniors. That was genius, red rag to a horde of bulls!*

Emmett looked down again at the laptop. The light hadn't changed. Couldn't Ross have made the screen come up with some sort of code? A timer? That's what happened in the movies, didn't it? You got a timer, and you suddenly whipped the device out just as it finished and before anyone else walked in.

'I'm going to make a call.'

That was Harlow. Emmett thought of his position in the room. If she stepped in through the door, she'd see him on the floor. He grabbed the laptop, and on his knees, worked his way round to behind her desk. He sat in underneath it, pulling the laptop onto his knees in front of him.

Footsteps entered the room, the door shut behind with vehemence. Emmett saw the chair at Harlow's desk being pulled out, and her feet suddenly appeared before him. As she sat down on the seat, a phone was picked up.

'Get me Macleod. Inverness.'

Emmett pulled himself in tight. The woman's feet were mere inches from him. If she reached out and kicked him, he could be in trouble.

Emmett sat, listening, as Harlow ran the riot act to Macleod. He couldn't hear the other end of the conversation, but Harlow was, in no uncertain terms, telling him that Emmett and Sabine needed to back off.

After a few minutes, she slammed the phone down and marched back out of her office. Emmett breathed a sigh of relief. She hadn't shut the door. His heart was pounding, but he noticed that the little device no longer had a red light on. He pulled it free from the laptop and dropped it in his pocket. Scrambling out on his knees, he replaced the laptop into the bag where he'd found it.

He dared not look up, though, in case anyone was looking back into Harlow's office. And he wondered if Sabine was going to be able to create more of a diversion. He took out his phone and texted Sabine, knowing it would set off the vibration in her pocket. As he did so, he could feel the sweat dripping down his face. He wiped it clear and crouched there for a moment. And then he heard it.

There was a crash, and Emmett didn't hesitate. Crouching down, he sprinted from the office round the corner and then became upright as he walked down the corridor beyond. He kept walking straight out of the station and into the car.

He sat there for several minutes until he saw a black-haired, tall figure emerge from the station. Sabine got into the car, started the engine, and drove off.

'You all right?' asked Emmett.

Sabine's hands were shaking. 'I flipped their coffee. I flipped the coffee tray. Did you hear it?'

'Heard it, all right.'

Sabine pulled the car over.

'Well?' asked Emmett. 'Did they suspect anything?'

'No, did you get the device?'

'We'll get it up to Ross. But what's the matter?'

'She took a call just before I left. Harlow just told me to leave in the end. But she was rattled. Not at me, but from the call she took. She was gunning for me, but then it all changed. She was desperate to leave. I got out before her. She was making for her coat.'

'You say desperate. She was—'

'She was spooked, Emmett. This call came in and she—'

A car drove past them, and Emmett noticed Sabine checking who was in it as it passed.

She shook her head. 'Not that one.'

'What do you mean, not that one?' asked Emmett.

A red car then drove past them. 'That one,' said Sabine. She waited until the car was a short distance ahead, indicated, and pulled out. 'She's rattled, and she's going somewhere.'

'Then we follow,' said Emmett. 'Good work. Don't lose her.'

Chapter 16

E mmett sat in the front seat of the car, staring at the long, if rather bland, building that comprised the hotel at the motorway services. Harlow had checked in there. A strange decision, considering she had departed in such a hurry.

Between the two of them, either Emmett or Sabine had watched the front of the building, and Harlow hadn't left. Her car was still sitting in the car park. No one had come or gone that they recognised. Emmett had taken the chance to call Ross, who had diverted Perry to pick up the USB device.

When Emmett returned to the car, allowing Sabine to get food, they wondered what was coming. The weather was not great, and it looked like it was going to get worse. Heavy snow was forecast. The temperature would drop well below freezing as well. The wind was also forecast to pick up. He wasn't looking forward to it.

The services stayed open until late, but as they got to the midnight hour, it was getting cold in the car. They didn't want to be getting in and out all the time and they parked at the furthest end of the car park. This was fine during the day, as cars were coming and going all the time. But now, the services were settling down; the cafe was closed, and it was quietening for the night. Staying incognito was becoming more difficult.

'Do you think anything's going to happen? Or are we just going to sleep in here?'

'All I've got's my big coat,' Emmett replied to Sabine. 'It's strange, isn't it? Out in Spain, feeling like I was going to sweat like a pig. Back here, and I'm frozen again.'

He saw Sabine smile at him.

'I think she'll be holed up for the night.'

'I don't,' said Emmett. 'She never went with any gear, did she? She didn't take up a room because of an investigation. She's been told to come here and wait for instructions. It must be somebody important. It must be whoever's in charge of whatever group or team that planned all of this.'

'I can't get my head around what's really happening,' said Sabine.

'And we won't until we find out who she's working for,' said Emmett. 'Macleod's right, it could be big.'

Around one a.m., Emmett was falling asleep when Sabine nudged him. 'There she is. She's going to her car.'

'Follow then, but easy, not too quick.'

DCI Harlow started her car, drove out of the car park, down towards the large roundabout that would lead her on to the motorway. Carefully, Sabine followed, but blasted heat through the car. It had misted up and Emmett was wiping down the windscreen with his forearm.

'Where do you think she's going?' said Sabine.

Pulling on to the motorway, she found the surface was clear, though there was white on either side. There was something about the snowy darkness, where you could always see the white beyond. However, there was so much cloud, the moonlight couldn't get through to brighten the dimness. Only the lights occasionally positioned at junctions brought a greater clarity to beyond the motorway.

It wasn't long before Harlow pulled off at a junction, heading out into the countryside. Sabine stayed well back, as the road was quiet, and then saw Harlow pull away, routing towards a quiet cottage.

'Go on past, and we'll pull up somewhere,' said Emmett.

The cottage was just about in view, as Sabine pulled off the road into a lay-by. She looked across at Emmett.

'Just a moment,' he said. He wrapped himself up in his large coat, got his binoculars out, and with Sabine, stepped out into the snow that was beyond the lay-by.

'What do you see?' asked Sabine, putting on her own large coat.

'She's gone inside. The car's sat there. Single light on in the cottage.'

'What do we do?' asked Sabine.

'We're getting close,' said Emmett. 'We should take a look over there. But we need to stay with the car too.'

'If she drives off again and we're over there, we'll not get back in time,' said Sabine. 'If one of us is with the car, we've got a chance to keep tailing her.'

'That's true,' said Emmett.

'Well, there's only one option, isn't there?' said Sabine. 'I'll go to the cottage. I'm much more geared up for that than you are. Here.' She handed him the keys.

'Take care,' said Emmett. 'No risks. Just watch.'

Sabine took off her large jacket and went into the boot of the car to pull out a black waterproof. She put a black hat on her head that matched her black jeans, but pulled on black waterproof trousers. Her hiking boots would be good enough. Then she pulled out a black scarf, wrapping it around her face as best she could.

Sabine was as dark as she could make herself and disappeared off into the snow. It may have been white and she may have been in black, but the darkness meant it would be hard to pick out her shape fully, as it melted into the night's shadows.

The wind was whipping hard now, and she couldn't hear much other than its own voice. She got close to the building and settled down behind a bush, trying to look carefully to see if anything was happening. Presumably there was no one inside, as there was only the one car. The light hadn't been on when they'd gone past initially, not until Harlow had stepped inside.

Sabine felt the vibration in her pocket and picked her mobile from her pocket. There was a message from Emmett. A black limo was on its way. She looked over and could see it coming down the long driveway to the cottage. Sabine put the phone away and tried to get closer.

There was a line of bushes close to the cottage, and she was able to sneak in behind them. The car would pull up maybe twenty feet from her, but if she got beyond the bushes, she was out in the open. Anyone stepping out of the house, would see her.

This was probably her limit, unless the coast became clearer.

The black limo drew up beside the house, and a chauffeur dressed in black stepped out, walked around the car, and then opened the back door. There was so little light that whoever got out was in shadow. The chauffeur also had a peaked cap pulled down, despite the darkness.

Sabine was struggling to identify either of them. Her phone

would never pick out anything but a grainy black in this light. She would need a proper camera, and she didn't have one on her. The chauffeur walked the man to the front door, which the chauffeur opened, and the man stepped inside.

There was no light coming from the hallway, the only light being from a window of presumably a living room or lounge or something of that ilk. Only the one light had ever come on. The chauffeur walked back to the car and sat inside, meaning Sabine couldn't get closer to the house without being seen. She hunkered down, wondering what to do. She daren't even risk the phone, in case its light was seen.

Sabine worked her way along the hedge, wondering if she could come round the back. She got down on her belly, crawling through the snow, feeling the icy cold touch her chin. The scarf she'd wrapped up around her was damp, wet from pristine white powder.

When she got up onto her knees behind a small bush, the wind whipped across her face. The cold scarf meant that the icy blast connected with her chin. She felt herself shiver. However, she could move from the bush and get up to the house without the limo driver seeing her. But she couldn't come round the front to the window. Instead, racing quickly, she made her way round to the back of the house.

There were no lights here. She peered in through windows and saw nothing, except a bland dining room, and then an empty room. Sabine knew that the wind was howling hard, and she walked back quickly to the bush she'd hidden behind. As she plunked herself down, she glanced back at the exterior of the house and noticed the limo driver walking around the exterior.

She wouldn't have heard him coming. Her heart raced as

she realised how close she'd been to disaster. Resolved now, she held her ground until he walked past around the house, and hopefully was heading back for the car. She crept back, staying among the bushes, until she was at her original point, from where she'd first seen the limo arrive. She wondered what Emmett was doing. Was he sitting watching with the binoculars?

Was there anyone else out there covering this limo? That wasn't unheard of. Someone would watch from a distance. Emmett hadn't texted anyway, so he either had nothing to tell her or he was otherwise occupied. The wind howled and Sabine froze, but then she saw the front door open.

Harlow stepped out with the man from the limo. They were animated, Harlow angry, but Sabine couldn't see the man's face. However, from the gestures of his hands, he clearly was not happy about something. Harlow looked afraid, and yet it was difficult because of the lack of light. The wind and the snow were also driving across her view, so she could only make generalisations.

They were now shouting, but the words were getting lost in the wind. And then one drifted past. 'Mackey.' Definitely, that was 'Mackey.' Sabine could feel her heart thumping inside. Whatever had gone on in Spain hadn't gone to their plan, clearly. She watched as the man turned away.

He did it quickly, almost unexpectedly, but what caught Sabine's eye was just past his head where he would have been. She saw a bit of the wall. It appeared to break off.

Sabine held her position, though, and watched as the man got into the limo. The chauffeur shut the door for him, and the limo drove off. Harlow stepped back inside, at which point Sabine turned and made her way quickly across the fields back to Emmett.

As she arrived, she saw he was bending down low and watching something through his binoculars.

'You got something?' she asked, trying not to raise her voice too loud, but also aware that he would struggle to hear her over the wind. Emmett didn't flinch, and she came up close to him. She crept even closer, speaking directly into his ear. 'Have you got something?' she said. He simply nodded, not speaking to her.

She leaned in close with a cocked ear, so he wouldn't have to take his eyes off whatever he was looking at.

'Gunman. I think he took a shot,' said Emmett.

His hand was pointing in front of him, and he passed the binoculars to Sabine. She looked and saw the gunman. He was down low and crouched, and she wasn't sure if Emmett hadn't pointed him out that she would have seen him.

'There was a shot,' said Sabine, more loudly now that she knew the gunman was a distance away. 'He took off a chunk of the wall, but clearly missed. I didn't even hear the shot.'

'I think he had a silencer on the rifle,' said Emmett. 'He didn't look to be too steady, though. He was struggling with the wind.'

'How are they here? Do you think we brought them here? Or did they follow her? Or him?'

'I don't know,' said Emmett. 'I didn't pick the gunman until after the limo was here. But that means nothing. It was difficult to trace the line of them in the dark.'

Sabine huddled up close to Emmett. She was feeling the cold, although the trip back from the house had warmed her up a little.

'What do we do?' asked Sabine.

134

'We watch the gunman. We can't follow the limo. It's gone. Harlow is still there. So, we wait until Harlow leaves. The only other option is to go to the gunman now. Maybe he's waiting for a shot at Harlow. Or maybe he's waiting for the limo to come back. Could you tell who he was shooting at?'

'The figure that was in the limo, I think. They turned suddenly. I think that's what the problem was.'

'This gunman might be from the group or the person who pushed us into this. Well, Harlow's part of the group covering up the story. Whatever the true story is.'

'Shall we call for back-up?' Sabine asked Emmett.

'No. Time it gets here, middle of the night. We can trace Harlow back with the car. The gunman's come out of nowhere. Their car isn't close.'

'I'll stay on him then,' said Sabine.

'She's coming out,' said Emmett suddenly. He was swinging the binoculars now between Harlow in the cottage and the gunman.

'Gunman's put the rifle away,' said Emmett. 'Clearly doesn't want Harlow. You get after the gunman. But keep a distance. I'll follow Harlow, see where she goes. If she goes back to the hotel at the motorway services, I'll come back to you.'

'Okay,' said Sabine. She jumped down from the lay-by out into the field again, skirting along hedgerows.

Sabine could see the gunman now. He had a bag slung over his shoulder; the rifle packed away into it. He was striking out across the fields. Sabine looked and saw Harlow's car disappearing back down the country roads. A distance behind it came Emmett in their car.

'Just keep your distance,' said Sabine, watching as the man ahead walked almost unbelievably across fields. He stood strong in the wind and didn't seem to think anyone was watching him. Soon she was able to pick up on his footprints and follow him from a slightly greater distance.

He was always just in view, but she stayed close to hedgerows to try to make sure she wasn't seen. How far would he go? And where? He must have had somewhere close to get back to. After all, you wouldn't camp out for the night in that wind. And maybe he had a car somewhere.

Sabine trudged forward, her arms wrapped around her as she continued to follow the man. She wished she had worn a big coat now, not the black waterproof she had on. Better for concealment, but far, far worse for keeping her warm.

Chapter 17

Sabine Ferguson shivered as she walked through the snowy fields. The wind was unrelenting, and the cold had formed a white across her black scarf that covered her face. It was damp, however, and so the bitterness was still coming through to her cheeks. The man up ahead with the gun, however, did not seem to slow down.

Sabine could see a barn in the distance. It was the middle of the night; she reckoned something like two o'clock, so the sky was still dark. But the outline of the barn could be made out. There looked like there was a road leading across to it, and she was unsure if the barn belonged to any building nearby. However, despite the cold, Sabine kept working through the snow, trying to keep her arms and legs moving. She would need shelter soon or she'd have to call off this pursuit.

She watched the man approach the barn, slide open a side door and step inside, closing the door behind him. Carefully, Sabine crept on through the snow until she got close to the barn as well. Thankfully, this side was sheltered from the wind.

She stepped close to the door the man had gone through. Inside, she could hear voices. However, there was still enough wind outside that she couldn't hear exactly what was being said. Turning around, she took a recce of the barn from the outside.

On her side of the barn were two doors that slid. The man had gone through one of them, and if she opened up either of them, Sabine wasn't sure that she wouldn't be seen. The barn was high, maybe fifteen feet, and so she walked to the end, where it met the road. Here, there were large gate-like doors. Again, opening one of those, or trying to, might alert those inside.

The other side of the barn, however, was just a brick wall. Going to the rear of the barn, Sabine could see a small opening at the top. It was shuttered but it had a metal ladder, that worked its way up to the shutters. Carefully, she climbed the ladder, thankful her hands were gloved, as she clambered up, snow covering the metal.

She went slowly, so as not to slip, and when she reached the wooden shutter at the top, she realised she could just about get through what was a small window. Sabine pulled at it gently, realising it could come free, and dragged it back. When she had a crack big enough to look through, she saw plenty of straw, and so opened the window more fully, clambering inside.

Slowly, she closed it behind her, hooking it shut and took a moment, lying in the straw on the other side of the window.

'They don't know we had a shot. They might see it tomorrow, they might see it another day, but it might just look like a chip off the building.'

'What do we do?' said a second voice. Both were male.

'Well, it doesn't matter that you failed. We'll get him another time. Thankfully, they seem to be sloppy, unlike those tracking them down.'

'I thought he might have gone off after the limo.'

'We can only hope. But you said that the woman was out there.'

'I saw a woman at the house, hiding behind the bush. She had her back to me, and she wouldn't have seen. I'm not sure if she would have heard the shot. Probably not in that wind. Unlikely she would have seen it.'

'Well, not to worry. We'll keep the cottage under observation. See if they come back. So close to a major blow, though. Could you identify him?'

'No, but he was the important one,' said the gunman. 'He clearly was someone Harlow was taking the instructions from. She was holed up for a long time in that hotel. Might still be holed up there.'

'Rest up anyway. You stay here while I find out what our next move is. Then I'll come back and pick you up. Easiest to keep that gun out of sight here. No one will come and you can sleep. Plenty of straw about.'

Sabine lay quietly, listening to the two men. Then she heard one move over towards the door. Quietly, she snuck forward on the straw, careful not to push any ahead of her. She was clearly up on a higher platform and from her vantage point, she could see that the platform didn't extend fully across the barn. So there would be a drop into the barn below. If she could get to the edge of the platform, she might see them. Sabine dragged herself forward. She heard the voices down below begin again.

'Wait a minute. How long am I going to be here? There's no food.'

'Well, I can drop you something, but I need to find out what's going on first. You might not even need it. It might only be a couple of hours.'

'It was kind of cold out there. You realise that, don't you?'

'You're getting paid well enough for it. So just accept it, okay?'

Sabine had slipped herself forward and was peering over the top of the platform she was on. Down below, she saw a man by the door. He turned back after opening the door, giving the man he was talking to a wave. She was hoping to glance a face, but there was a balaclava on, and then the man was gone.

Would the man below have one on? He probably did while he was walking along in that snow; something to cover his face. You couldn't have done without it, so hard was the weather blowing into them. Also, if you were sitting behind a trigger, you wouldn't want anything to disturb your shot. He surely would have been covered, although now he was alone, maybe that would change. She wouldn't have fancied trying to sleep in a balaclava. It'd be too warm.

Sabine leaned over and eventually was able to peer beneath the platform. The gunman was lying now amongst the straw. He had his back to her, but she could see he still had what looked like a balaclava on. She slowly crept back, lay on her back, and took her phone out of her pocket.

Quickly, she texted a message to Emmett explaining the situation. Sabine lay back there, wondering about the next move. She could try to apprehend the man, but she'd want backup, at least Emmett, to be there. She had a set of handcuffs tucked away inside her waterproofs, and she could certainly handcuff him. But if no backup was coming and instead, the man's colleague returned, she'd be in trouble. And these were people you didn't want to have trouble with. After all, they'd just taken a pot shot at someone. They didn't even know who it was.

Her phone wasn't on vibrate anymore. She'd switched it to silent. But it lit up when Emmett gave his response. Harlow had gone to bed in the hotel that she'd occupied for most of that afternoon. Emmett was currently sitting out front, back in the car park.

Holding the phone in front of her, she messaged back that she would apprehend the gunman. She waited, and it was only twenty seconds later when the reply came.

'Don't. Wait for backup. Wait for help.' After messaging back with an 'OK,' Sabine lay back and wondered what she should do next. If the man left the building, she wasn't in the greatest place to follow him, but she couldn't go down to the floor below. If she went back outside, and he didn't leave for a while, she could be out there in the snow for how long?

Sabine was still cold from being outside, although now, she certainly was warmer than during her trek. She had packed some of the straw around her, and it was acting like a large duvet. Slowly, she was getting more feeling than she had before. Emmett said wait, though. So wait, she would.

Sabine started trolling through the case, wondering how they'd got to this position. She also was worried if there was something behind the scenes, how easy would it be to bring it to the fore? Macleod was a big name, but even he was far from the top dog. Did he have enough friends?

That wasn't his style. His previous days down in Glasgow, as far as she could tell from being around those who had worked with him, he was cold with people. Not warm, and far from how good he was now. But she'd worked with him in assisting Clarissa, and he certainly was clever enough. She feared for Emmett, though. He seemed to have a dogged determination about him. He made most of his decisions based on a quiet sensibility.

But with this case? His determination to sort this out was in overdrive. Maybe things should be left alone, she wondered. After all, what did it matter? Of course, it mattered if this operation was still ongoing. Were there people there to take out those who broke the law and got away with it continually? There was a secret service for that, wasn't there? But even they operated within parameters.

She didn't like the idea of arbitrary execution. She didn't like the clandestine side that was clearly being portrayed here. Sabine had enjoyed the Arts team and loved her artwork. She got to see some terrific pieces. Yes, Clarissa took a bit of getting used to, but she hadn't looked to race into other types of crime.

In fact, why had she come? Well, she'd come because Emmett was here and Emmett had asked her. That was the key thing, wasn't it? Emmett had asked her. She remembered being younger, and a boyfriend had asked her to transfer down to England. He was going for work, and they were fairly close, but she'd said no. She was sticking with Glasgow.

Emmett wasn't even a boyfriend. Emmett was—well, he was a friend, and he was a good friend, a close friend, but they didn't speak that much, that closely. Most of their talk was about comics and games and role-playing. It wasn't about, well, what people who were really fond of each other talked about.

Well, they didn't talk always, did they? Some people. Some people did very little talking. Showed their affection in other ways.

She sat up with a start as the door down below opened and then closed again.

'Just got off with him. ' It was the man who had left returning. 'He wants you to stay here. Your money's being transferred over. But they want you to lie tight here, at least for twenty-four hours. Don't get on the move. Just in case the man in the limo realises he was shot at. They can move resources. You'll be safe here.'

'That's not the deal. I get my money, and I go. Okay? I'm not up for that. Why would I wait here? You know I'm here. Somebody could come and pop me off. Transfer the money over. I'm going.'

'Look mate, I'm just a messenger,' said the man who had come in. 'But he told you to wait here. Now I'm off.'

Sabine heard the door being slid back open giving a loud howl of the wind before being closed again. She crept forward, and she heard the man getting up. Looking over her platform of straw, she saw him stand up and put his bag around him. She heard the word 'arseholes' being mentioned. And then the man wandered over to the corner. She heard him unzip. He was going to take a leak.

This was her opportunity, she thought. She couldn't wait for Emmett. She got up onto her feet, snuck along the top of the platform, and then let herself hang down from it. The man was in the far corner, underneath the platform, urinating on the wall. Sabine let herself drop four feet behind him. She landed so quietly, the man didn't even flinch. Slowly, she crept up on him. She stood there, watching as he whistled to himself.

He finished, and was tucking himself back in when she moved quickly up behind him. She'd have to be fast, and Sabine took a set of handcuffs out. As he went to turn, she grabbed his arm, slapping cuffs on one wrist, and then grabbing and slapping them on the other. The man went to kick back at her, but she shoved him forward, and he bounced into the wall. He looked like he was about to tumble, and she hit him with a punch to the stomach.

The man doubled over, and Sabine pushed down on top of his shoulders, telling him to stay on his knees. Hopefully, Emmett could come soon. Sabine reached down, picked out her mobile phone again, and sent a message. He'd be annoyed that she'd acted without him, but the gunman was about to leave and anyway, she now had him in custody. She reached down and pulled off the balaclava. She was staring at short brown hair at the back of his head and a tattoo of some sort of an eagle at the base of the neck.

'Just stay there,' said Sabine. 'Don't move. We're not going anywhere.' The man laughed. 'I mean it,' said Sabine. 'You're not going anywhere. We've got plenty of questions to ask you. Plenty of—'

An immense pain formed in the back of her head. She'd clearly been struck by something. As she tumbled down, she looked up and saw the masked face above her of her attacker. He was holding a small cudgel, and she toppled, going sideways before her head cracked on the floor.

Everything went dark.

Chapter 18

Her head was pounding. There was blackness everywhere. But the pain was constant. Slowly, she felt her arms and the rest of her body. She reached out and could feel the straw.

Sabine was lying awkwardly on her front, half twisted, so that her hips were upright in a line from the floor and her feet were lying one on top of each other. But she was almost lying face down from the torso up. In fact, she was twisted with the arms spread out. It just meant more pain, although it was so incredibly minor compared to what was ringing in her head.

Sabine pushed herself upright and got into a sitting position. The barn had some natural light streaming in through the upstairs window. In the evening, there had been a light. There must have been a dim electric one, because underneath, the platform had been lit up. She had come down and seen the man.

It was strange that this bothered her. But she looked up and around and could see a small emergency light. That must have been what had caused things to be lit up. Those lights were so bright when everything else was dark. But in the daylight—it was daylight, wasn't it?

Gradually, Sabine worked herself up until she was standing. She reached round, running her hands through her black hair to feel the bump at the back of her head. It had been a good one, but it hadn't broken the skin. It was now she realised that something had come off her when she stood up. Beside her was an orange bivvy bag. Why was that there?

Looking at it, it appeared to be brand new. Slowly, she searched her pockets. Nothing had been removed. Her phone was still there. She pulled it out and pressed the button, but nothing came on. Was it dead? Had they taken a battery? Then she held the button in, felt a slight vibrate, and the loading up screen came on. Somebody had switched it off.

She entered her code, and soon the phone was functioning normally. She wondered at first what to do, but saw missed calls coming in. They were from Emmett. She called him back straight away. It took a moment for him to answer, but when he did, she could hear the relief in his voice.

'Sabine! Where are you?'

'I think I'm okay,' she said. 'I'm still in the barn. Yes, I'm still in the barn.'

'What happened?'

'I went to apprehend him. He was leaving, and I got him. I put handcuffs on him. And then somebody hit me. I went out completely. My head's aching.'

'So, how did you get free?' asked Emmett.

'I didn't. I'm here in the barn. There's a bivvy bag. They just left me. Whoever did it just left me.'

'Where are you exactly?'

'Hang on a minute,' she said. Sabine went into the phone's map function and found the coordinates of her position. She relayed them to Emmett.

'I've been driving round and round since last night. Decided I had to leave Harlow because I hadn't heard from you. I was about to canvass everybody else. I do want to try to find out where you were in case . . . well, we don't know who we can trust at the moment.'

'I'm okay, Emmett,' she said. 'But it's weird. We're being played. We're definitely being played. But somebody wants us to keep going. I think it might even be the ones who tried to kill that man.'

'I'll be there in a minute. Let me have a look. Yes, I'm only a couple of miles away, maybe ten, fifteen minutes max. Just stay there, yes?'

Sabine wasn't going to just stay there. Where was she, exactly? She'd trudged through all those fields to the barn. Yes, she had coordinates, but what was around here?

She walked over to the door that the man had come through the previous night. It was open and slid back to one side. She felt a blast of cold air. There was no snow falling now, but there was a modest wind blowing. Stepping out into the deep snow on the ground, she saw a beautiful landscape of white. There was nothing around the barn, however. No tracks.

Whatever tracks were made must have been filled in overnight by the snow. Not even any tyre prints to go on. Nothing. She tried to see if anyone was watching the place, but could see no one with her bare eyes. *Emmett has the binos*, she thought. She hesitated on seeing a car approaching but it looked the right colour for their car.

Soon, she saw Emmett drive in. The car pulled up, making two lines behind it in the fresh snow. Emmett jumped out, running over to her.

'I'm okay,' she said. But he flung his arms around her, pulling her close. She pulled him tight back. 'I'm okay, Emmett.'

He didn't let go. 'It was too close,' he said. 'If they'd wanted to. Just like at the bus stop.'

Eventually, Sabine pushed him back a bit, telling him she was fine. 'Paracetamol,' she said. 'I need some paracetamol. You got some in the car?'

'Of course,' he said. Emmett disappeared into the car and came back with paracetamol and a bottle of water. Sabine drank some of the water, throwing the tablets down with it.

'How are you feeling? Apart from the sore head,' said Emmett.

'I am frozen solid.'

'Get in,' he said. 'We'll go back and see if Harlow's still there.'

Once in the car, Emmett turned the heating up, and by the time they'd reached the services where the hotel was located, the car was a positive sauna. However, Harlow's car was gone.

'Damn it,' said Sabine. 'She was our link in.'

'You're safe,' said Emmett. 'I came to get you and now you're safe. That's far more important. Let's get some food. You must be starving.'

Sabine nodded, and Emmett parked the car in the car park, before they headed off to the cafe. He ordered two large breakfasts, and they sat down with coffee, eating and drinking, but saying very little. Once they'd had their fill, however, Emmett stared across at her.

'We might have to monitor Harlow. I think we need to see some other people.'

'How do you mean?' asked Sabine.

'I mean, we have to go back. I'm thinking about Anne Matthews. Anne Matthews was dead keen to sort out avenging her husband, see what the true story was going on behind it.

If she's in any way like him, she'll have found something out. We're getting played and I'm not sure she's not part of that. She's not on either side, or at least we need to find out if she is. I'm thinking I might open up to her, tell her the way things are. If she's not on either side, she might help much more than she did before. However, if she is, she might give something away under pressure.'

'It sounds good. Why don't we head for Pitlochry? You can get Macleod on the phone,' said Sabine.

'I need to meet up with him. I'm thinking that the more I involve him, the more it will call things out. If we don't, we're going to end up just chasing around. We're going to be led on the merry dance. We're being used to find people. If we bring Macleod in more, well, I think those higher up will react. We need to change the circumstances we're in, one way or another.'

'Head for Pitlochry, then, once we finish here.'

'No,' said Emmett. 'We head for a car hire. We need to get another car. A car for you, because you're going to sit and watch Harlow. Get back over to the Glasgow station, and see if you can pick her trail up. And do not let her out of your sight once you have her.'

'Because? You think she's going to disappear?'

'Look,' said Emmett, 'from what we gathered at the cottage when she met the man from the limo, they weren't happy. She could end up running. Or with these types of people, she could end up not existing. It looks like they may have killed Isbister. They're not behind the door here. We were going to be wiped out.

'She's liable to just run if things get too much. Harlow knows who they are. She knows more details than most other people.

149

They could just cut her loose. Just say that's that. You need to keep an eye on her. And if they come for her, it might show us someone else. But I don't want to put lots of tails on her. We need to keep this as quiet as possible.'

'I don't like it, Emmett,' said Sabine. She reached forward, grabbed his hand, holding tightly in hers. 'I'm very fond of you. You're a good friend. We've already come close on this one. This isn't our fight. This isn't—'

'Of course it's our fight,' said Emmett. 'It looks like the police have been compromised. It's not right. We can't let it stand, no more than you can let a killing stand. People have died, and it hasn't been resolved properly. It hasn't been looked into fully. It's up to us because we're officers and it's what we do.'

'But Macleod didn't even—'

'The trouble with Macleod is, people hold him up on a pedestal. Macleod this, Macleod that. The man Macleod is now is not the man Macleod was. I'm not the same person I was ten years ago. You're not the same woman. We don't just get older. We change.

'He's been challenged. He knows he should have done more back then. Seoras knows he should have found a way out. But maybe he didn't have the capacity. Maybe he was under the cosh. Maybe whatever. It doesn't matter. The thing is, that there may be a renegade group still existing. And in finding out what happened to Isbister, we can find out if there was a group, a major miscarriage of justice, or if we had a dirty side to our force. Knowing that's a possibility makes me want to react, makes me want to do things. You're too good a cop not to do it, too.'

'We don't want to get lost in this, Emmett,' said Sabine. 'You forget where I came from. I watched people try to stand up and make my land a good land. People died.'

'Then we'd better be darn good,' said Emmett. He picked up his phone and called Macleod.

'Seoras here. How are you?'

'Are you okay with being updated?' asked Emmett. 'You need to understand what's going on. I need to meet you as well.'

'Why?' asked Macleod.

'We got in and we've sent up the data stick to Ross; however, we also followed Harlow. Sabine got a hunch that she was annoyed after a phone call. We tailed her to the cottage on the outskirts of Glasgow in the middle of the night, meeting someone who pulled up in a limo. While there, they had a discussion inside the house.

'When they came out, somebody took a pot shot at them. Sabine followed the gunman, got knocked out, but they left her. Didn't tie her up, in fact made sure she was okay by the looks of it. Harlow's disappeared back and I think we're going to keep tabs on her. Sabine's going to do that. I'm heading for Pitlochry. I want to talk to Anne Matthews. We need a different angle. We need to change what's happening here and stop getting jerked about.'

'I'll come to Pitlochry,' said Macleod. 'It'll take me a couple of hours to get out of here, but then I'll meet up with you. You're going to need some backup, anyway. You can't have you two of you running around singly, won't work.'

'And I want you down here,' said Emmett. 'I want you in the firing line. I want people's attention brought in. Time to make a head-to-head happen with these people. Otherwise, we're going to get slowly picked off by one side or the other. If things have been in place for a long time, like I possibly suspect, then the only way to bring it to a head is to have something big happen. You're the one they didn't want down here. Or at least the ones trying to cover up whatever's happened. Those who wanted it brought out into the light wanted to get you to do it and make it big. Like, you scuppered their plans, throwing me into the mix.'

'It's almost like I planned that, isn't it? It's in my blood. But I agree with you. It's time to get things changed. Time to make the playing field look somewhat different. I'll see you soon. However, you need to know something.'

'What?' asked Emmett. 'Has Ross got in through that stick already?'

'No, he's not come back on that,' said Macleod. 'But there's a report from the Spanish police. There's a British man dead in Alicante, by the name of Donald Mackey.'

'Covering tracks. We'd better keep a close eye on Harlow,' said Emmett, 'because she, at the moment, is an open link they might just want to close.'

'I'll see you later today,' said Macleod. 'Take care.'

Emmett closed down the call and turned to Sabine. 'He's on board with it. Let's go do it.'

They stood up, but once again, Sabine grabbed Emmett by the hand.

'Take flippin' care out there, okay?' she said.

'And you,' said Emmett.

He walked away from the cafe, Sabine in tow. He'd already sent her off on her own once. She was lucky to have not died. And he was struggling to come to terms with what could have been. Now he was sending her off again. He swallowed hard. It was the right decision, but felt so very wrong. Whatever he thought of his best friend.

Chapter 19

As Emmett drove up towards Pitlochry, with either side of the road lined with trees set back deep into the mountainside, and the snow lying all around, he couldn't help but worry about leaving Sabine behind. He had to change the course of this investigation. Things had to be brought to the fore. They'd had two incredibly close calls—Sabine being left overnight in the barn when anything could have happened to her, and the pot shot at them out in Spain.

You could also add the gunman in Emmett's hotel room in Pitlochry, who had chosen not to fire. Emmett was glad that at least one faction involved in this case didn't want them dead. One side was pushing them forward, the other pulling them back.

Identifying what each faction was, however, was proving difficult. He had no actual evidence on Harlow. Yes, she'd led them down the garden path. Somebody had taken a shot at her friend in the limo, but what had she done that was actually illegal? Nothing so far, Emmett thought. And if he went through traditional channels, trying to dig up the past, both Sabine and he could end up compromised.

Bringing Macleod into the mix was bound to stir up things.

Having him come down to work with them would make people think they were getting closer. More drastic action would be taken. But with more drastic action, maybe other parties would reveal themselves.

That's what Emmett hoped.

But first off, he was to see Anne Matthews. At their first meeting, the woman had been reticent to offer any information and he wondered if she would give more this time. He was prepared to open up more. He thought he would explain the issues he was having. Her husband had been a journalist, someone ready to explore the wrongness on both sides of the equation.

It was hard sometimes when you were a policeman to think about those who were not pristine examples of law enforcement. You didn't like to think that of your colleagues. But it appeared in this case that's what had happened. Anne's husband had been a man who would have brought that up. But he wouldn't have let the darker side of criminality go, either. He'd have shone a light everywhere. Whether he did this for notoriety, money, or whatever, it wasn't really Emmett's concern. Maybe he could appeal to Anne to be that person, to help the memory of her husband.

As he pulled into the driveway, Emmett took a deep breath. He didn't have Sabine with him. She wasn't just a calming influence on him, but a friendly influence to people. Emmett never really managed that. For some reason, people didn't see him as a friendly soul. Not outright nasty or anything. It's just that they didn't warm to him easily. People warmed to Sabine.

He understood. She had the looks for it. The long hair, tall figure. A shapely figure, too. Emmett wasn't immune to the attraction of women. And certainly, there was a lot about

Sabine he liked in the physical sense. But he really liked her for the person she was. That shone through. Whenever she spoke to someone, they didn't tend to back away. They didn't wonder what was going on in Sabine's head.

Maybe that was Emmett's problem. Maybe he looked like he was thinking too much. He didn't try to do that. It's just how he worked.

When he knocked on the door and it was opened, Anne Matthews stood before him with a frown on her face.

'I told you before,' she said. 'I'm not telling you anything. All right. I told you the basics. We're not going any further. I don't trust any of you.'

'That's understood,' said Emmett. 'I don't trust anyone either.'

Anne stood and looked at him for a moment, before there came a shout over her shoulder.

'Everything all right, Mum?'

'It's one of those detectives, the one I told you about, looking into your father's death. Only he's here without the good-looking one.'

Emmett gave a slight shrug of his shoulders. If she had said it the other way around, Sabine would have been rightly annoyed, and he could understand why. He looked over Anne Matthews's shoulder but fought the garishness of her outfit. She was wearing another one of her large summer dresses, despite the winter chill.

The woman's jowly cheeks, framed by that long blonde hair, impeded him seeing where the voice had come from.

'Do you want me to deal with him?'

'I don't want anybody to deal with him,' said Anne. 'I'm just going to shut the door on him.'

She reached over and grabbed the door, and started to close it, but Emmett put his foot in the way.

'Don't,' he said. The woman reacted badly, as if she was ready to slam the door again, this time on his foot, but Emmett put his hand forward and said, 'Don't, please.'

'And why the hell not?' raged Anne.

'Your husband seemed to think that there was coercion going on. More than that, I think he was on to the idea that certain elements within the police force were trying to get rid of the McIntoshes. Not in a, how should we put it, legal way?'

'That's not exactly uncommon knowledge, is it? Most people could come up with that.'

'Well, I don't claim to be taking credit for that, but as I've gone to investigate, I've had somebody trying to push me and give me directions,' said Emmett. 'I've got other people trying to lead me off into paths. I've been shot at, had my room ransacked. My partner was knocked out. Now, some people are trying to protect us and want us to get to the bottom of what was occurring; others aren't. There's a real dichotomy going on. I'm wondering where you would stand on that. After all, your husband paid for what he tried to do. Maybe I could finish his investigation, maybe I could—'

'Is this him, Mum?' asked a voice from behind Anne Matthews.

'Yeah, babes, this is him.'

Emerging behind Anne Matthews was a woman with long, thick, wavy dark hair. She was as big as her mother, not unshapely but with full curves. Emmett wasn't a big man—he was stuck in a small frame and he was dwarfed by the two women. A pair of gold earrings hung from the new woman's ears and she looked heavily made up.

'Mum said she didn't want to talk to you,' said the woman. 'I'll deal with it, Mum. Off you go.'

Anne Matthews turned away and walked back inside the house, leaving the other woman there.

'I take it you're her daughter,' said Emmett.

'Emma Matthews. You are—?'

'Detective Inspector Emmett Grump. I'm looking into the case that involves Gavin Isbister, the man they thought killed your father and then committed suicide.'

'Isbister didn't do it. Everybody knows Isbister didn't do it.'

'Talk to me then,' said Emmett.

'Outside,' said the woman. She turned and closed the door behind her, then followed Emmett out onto the driveway.

'My mother, she's not, well, it's been such a strain on her, you know.'

'And for you? You're her daughter, after all.'

'Yes, there's been pressure, but I got away, didn't I? I got out of here. The thing was that, even after it was done, there was constant pressure from the police trying to tell Mum not to talk too much about the case. They were worried that Mum knew stuff that me Da knew. He wasn't like that. Me Da wanted to make sure that his work kept a distance from the family because if people thought Mum knew what he knew, she could get killed for it one day. He made a clear distinction. When he was talking to the McIntoshes, he said that only he would know anything. Mum wouldn't know.'

'And this pressure came from who?' asked Emmett.

'It was the murder squad, Isbister's bosses.'

'Harlow? Possibly a detective sergeant, detective constable at the time. Was there a Harlow? A woman?'

Emma shook her head. 'I don't remember her, not that name.

157

There were a couple of women, of course, but I don't remember them, well, they weren't talking to us. They were lower level, uniform, most of them.'

'It's important.' He pulled out a photograph of DCI Harlow and showed it to Emma Matthews. The woman took it off him and looked at it for a moment.

'Oh, I remember her; oh, yes.'

'So, she was here. She came round?'

'Not exactly. No, she's not police. She was, well, I remember it exactly because I was sorting out the last arrangements with the funeral directors and she was there, in the building, talking to them.'

'This was when your father was buried, was it?'

'No, he hadn't been buried at that point. They were going to bury him. It was two days before. No, a day before,' she said. 'That woman was there. I thought she was with another family or something. Or maybe she was just doing business. You know, we weren't the only ones that were bereaved at that time. Other people had rather less sensational bereavements.'

'Are you sure it's her?' asked Emmett.

'Well, she'd have been younger. But look at those eyes. You'll not forget that. Yeah, it was her. Slightly different figure. That's fuller. But it was her.'

'And you don't recall her giving a name or saying anything?' asked Emmett.

'She was talking to different people. I was there signing off, making sure the undertakers knew everything about me Da, what was going to happen with him, where he was getting buried. Just finalising all those details that you have to do. And she was in the background, talking to the owner, I believe.'

'That's very interesting,' said Emmett. 'That's DCI Harlow.'

'And she's who?' asked Emma.

'That I'm still trying to work out,' said Emmett. 'I don't think she was on the case back in the day.'

'Mum said it was Macleod and Isbister. Macleod was taken off. There were a few others came in, but it was mainly Isbister until it all went wrong and me Da was dead.'

'Well,' said Emmett, 'Macleod has taken an interest in the case again. He was taken off it before your father died. He was investigating McCollum's murder—'

'You know, me Da never had a love for the McIntoshes, but he struggled,' said Emma. 'He struggled with what was going on. He would have loved to have given the evidence that would have put the McIntoshes behind bars. But he said something more was happening, more severe, to my mother. And that's where he left it. He left the wall between us. Made sure we didn't know so that nobody else would come later on. He made it well known. I don't think that would work these days, would it? You wouldn't have that sort of gentlemanly, 'Oh, my family know nothing; kill me, but don't touch them.''

'I don't know,' said Emmett. 'I've never wanted to threaten people like that.'

'If you hear anything, I'd love to know more,' said Emma. 'Because me Da's the one who suffered for it all. I'd love to see someone put behind bars for what they did to him.'

'I'll see what I can do,' said Emmett. He turned away and got back into his car.

Emmett drove out of the driveway and back into Pitlochry, where he sat in a coffee shop and placed a phone call to Macleod.

'I'll be down soon. I'm just tidying up,' said Macleod.

'Fair enough,' said Emmett. 'I'll see you later. I'm off to see the undertakers. Emma Matthews, the daughter of Simon and Anne Matthews, told me she believed DCI Harlow was there in the undertaker's after her father died. I thought Harlow wasn't on the case. Why would she have been in Pitlochry, never mind at the undertaker's?' said Emmett.

'She wasn't. She wasn't meant to be there. You usually knew where everybody was and she wasn't. She was meant to be back in Glasgow,' said Macleod.

'Seems strange to me,' said Emmett.

'Are you sure it's her, though? What age would this Emma woman have been?' asked Macleod.

'Teens?' said Emmett.

'DCI Harlow's changed a lot,' said Macleod, 'even from back when I knew her. She's a fair bit older.'

'I think our witness can turn round and reckon on somebody being a bit older. She's not five.'

'Oh,' said Macleod, 'but it's not concrete. It won't be watertight if she identifies her.'

'Nothing's watertight in this,' said Emmett. 'You don't seriously think we're going to get some sort of conviction at the end of it? I just want to get to the end of it and come out the other side. We're walking a bad line here. Two forces. I just hope that they're able to hold back until we can solve it. While I want to draw them out, I don't want them to take serious action—action that can end in death.'

'You always have to run the wire,' said Macleod. 'The older they go, the deeper the secrets too. Cold cases. They hit people out of the blue. They react stronger to them sometimes. It's when you learn that there isn't any real forgive and forget from most people.'

'I will check out the undertakers. See if anybody remembers

her being there. Because if she was there, she must have done something. Interfered somehow.'

'I understand that,' said Macleod. 'Be careful, though, and don't run into anything.'

'Run into anything?' said Emmett.

'They laid out a plan for you all along. You ended up in Spain at their behest. You nearly ended up dead. And you've noticed I'm pushing you on through. Take your time and think through properly. Make sure you keep in contact with Sabine. Too easy for her to disappear at the moment.'

'She's wise enough. She'll stay clear,' said Emmett. 'I look forward to seeing you later.'

He closed the call and drank the last of his coffee. Harlow? Harlow, he knew was deep in this. And lo-and-behold, she appears again. But at the funeral directors, around when Matthews was being buried. If that's the case, what was she doing there? Matthews got buried. He was already dead. If she'd done something to cause that, the last place she'd be is there. He shook his head. She must have been there for another reason. Must have been. But what? Emmett needed to find out.

Chapter 20

E mmett parked the car in the middle of Pitlochry and walked down its older streets, looking for the funeral directors. There was a modern-looking front on the building, more the trend these days. Emmett wondered why that was. He'd have thought that the best thing for funeral directors was to look established, because grievers wanted people who could take care of things.

No fuss. Done with, well, not aplomb, not style, but with sincerity. With decency. That's what you wanted, wasn't it? Respect. Some of the more modern fronts of the funeral directors didn't portray that. Emmett thought that was a mistake, in so much as he ever thought about funeral directors. This one, however, looked very modern, but when Emmett entered, he was greeted by a mature woman, who certainly looked like she meant business.

Her hair was pulled back tight, and though grey, with bits of white in it, she was by no means that old. Her thick glasses, though, gave her an air of no-nonsense, and Emmett decided he would pull out his warrant card, so that he wouldn't be fobbed off. He knew that if he travelled about in jeans, t-shirts, and jumpers that were often advertising gaming conventions, he wouldn't always get taken seriously.

But Macleod said he was better in his everyday garb than he would be in a shirt and tie. Emmett just got on with it.

'Excuse me,' said Emmett. 'My name is Acting Detective Inspector Emmett Grump. I'd like to speak to the owner, please.'

'I'm afraid that Mrs Anderson is not available at the moment.'

'Oh, can I ask where she is?'

'Holiday. Winter sun. The rest of us can handle here. So off she went. Apparently you get the better prices. How can I help you, though?' asked the woman.

'I'm looking to speak to someone who was here maybe twenty-five years ago.'

'Well, there wouldn't be anybody in this building,' said the woman. 'Mrs Anderson took over the business fifteen years ago.'

'Do you remember who from?' asked Emmett.

'I wasn't here myself, but it's always been John Ferguson in town. Well-established business before Mrs Anderson took it over.'

'Any idea where I would find Mr Ferguson now?'

'That's a rather sad story. Mr Ferguson's wife died approximately five years ago, and he went gradually downhill. He's been in a home for the last three years, I think. I can't be exact on the dates. It's hearsay more than actual knowledge. A bit of gossip, if you will, Inspector.'

'Well, sometimes gossip is true,' said Emmett. 'Where would the home be, do you know?'

'Yes, it's just on the way out towards the A9. Look on the right-hand side.'

'Has it got a name?' asked Emmett.

'Oh, sorry,' she said, almost embarrassed. 'They worked hard on it. It's called Pitlochry Care Home.'

Emmett nearly burst out laughing. 'Well, it does exactly what it says on the tin, then.'

He thanked the woman and left, returning to his car. Snow was falling again. As he reached the care home, its rather splendid gardens were blanketed in white. In summer, it must be good for the residents to get out because there were picnic benches. Places where those who couldn't get elsewhere could still obviously enjoy nature. Emmett parked up and came through to the reception area. The home looked rather large and there was a young girl sitting behind the desk who looked up at him.

'What's the name of the loved one?' she asked.

'Not a loved one,' said Emmett.

'Well, we don't judge,' said the young girl. She had rather a good sense of decorum, given her age, Emmett thought. But he didn't have time for this.

'I'm Acting DI Emmett Grump,' he said, pulling out his warrant card. 'I'm looking for John Ferguson.'

'Ah,' said the woman. 'You may be too late.'

The hairs on Emmett's neck were raised. 'Too late?' he said. 'Why?'

'I'm afraid that Mr Ferguson hasn't been well for the last three, four months. He's probably not going to be with us by the end of the day, if he hasn't already gone.'

'I need to see him,' said Emmett. 'It is important.'

The young woman picked up a phone, spoke to someone, and then turned back, smiling at him. 'Angela will be with you in a moment. She's looking after his care.'

Emmett sat down, but only briefly, as a rather strong-looking woman came round the corner. She had brown hair down to her shoulders, but what she didn't have was a smile.

'Is this absolutely necessary?' asked Angela.

'Forgive me, I'm Acting DI Emmett Grump. Yes, it is. It's to do with a murder case. I need to speak to him.'

'He's in and out, to a large degree. I'm not sure what you'll get from him, or if it will even make any sense.'

'Then we need to hurry,' said Emmett. 'I do need to speak to him.'

'Don't distress him,' said Angela. 'Distress him and I'll throw you out.'

Emmett looked at the woman. She looked like she could throw him out. Emmett wasn't that strong, but then again, he used his brain to work things out, not his fists. He certainly wouldn't be able to use his fists against this woman. She had that matronly look about her, the old-style ones, the ones that took no nonsense—grabbed you by the ear and flung you out of the ward.

'If we can,' said Emmett. 'I'm sorry, but it really is important.'

The woman turned, told Emmett to follow her, and then marched through various corridors and up a couple of flights of stairs. There was a single room towards the back of the building where the lights were down low.

'Is there any family?' asked Emmett as she opened the door.

'Not here. They've been contacted. They've been back and forward the last lot of months. This isn't the first time we've thought he's going. But this time he's going. He'll not come back from this one.'

'Are you absolutely sure?' asked Emmett.

'Inspector, I don't tell you how to do your job. I don't question your opinion that you need to talk to him. So please, don't question mine when I say he won't be here by the end of the day.'

'Of course,' said Emmett. 'My apologies.'

He was led on into a dark room. A bed, tastefully dressed with a quilt and blankets, contained a man whose neck and head were the only things appearing from underneath the covers. He was turned to one side, and his breathing was heavy and laboured. His hair was grey and looked greasy, but he was shaved, nose hairs trimmed, Emmett noticed.

'John,' said Angela. 'John?'

'Yes? What?' said the man, his breathing hoarse.

'I've got an Acting DI Emmett Grump. Says he needs to speak to you. Says it's important.'

'Huh,' said the man, more of a grunt than anything else. Angela stepped back and waved Emmett in. He thought she might leave the room, but instead she stood behind him. Oh well, he thought. Can't help. Can't hurt. And if she works here, she's been here for a while.

Emmett got down on his knees, close up to the man's ear. 'I'm Emmett,' he said. 'John, I need you to remember something for me. I need you to remember when you were a funeral director.'

'Yeah,' said the man. 'Director. Job. It was my job,' he said, croaking.

'I need you to remember back to when you buried a man. His name was Simon Matthews.'

'Matthews,' said the dying man. 'Matthews.'

And then there was silence, except for that breathing, deep but staccato. Emmett wasn't sure if he'd fallen asleep. He turned to look at Angela. She held her hand up, telling him to remain. Emmett turned back. There was something being said by John. He leaned in, his ear now right in front of the man's mouth.

'Fuss,' he said. 'Lots of fuss.'

'Yes,' said Emmett. 'Do you remember a woman called Harlow?'

'No,' said the man.

'Do you remember burying Simon Matthews?'

'Fuss,' came the croaky voice again. 'They were still examining. Just before we were to bury him, had to be quick, couldn't get the warrant, so funeral went ahead.'

'Who?' asked Emmett. 'Who had to examine him?'

'Forensic.'

'Who?'

'Remember, can't remember.'

'How many?' asked Emmett.

'Two. They sealed the coffin. The coffin was sealed for us. We had sealed it, but they sealed it again.'

'When?' asked Emmett.

'When they'd finished. They were, they were—'

'Who were? Man? Woman?'

'Two men. Then we buried him. We took him in the car and buried him. It was okay. Didn't stop things. It was a difficult time.'

The breathing suddenly became even more laboured. There was a start from the man, and Angela came down beside Emmett.

'John,' said Emmett, 'are you still with us?'

John continued to breathe, rasping, hoarse, and Angela reached over, checking him.

'Is he—?'

Angela put her finger to her lips and pulled Emmett back a

bit. She whispered in his ear.

'I don't know. He's obviously still alive, because he's still breathing, but towards the end, sometimes they just—well, it's about all they're doing. But they say their hearing's the last to go, so he may be hearing you and not able to respond.'

Emmett got down again on his knees. 'John, if you can hear me—'

'Nearly wrong. Nearly went wrong.'

'Why?' asked Emmett.

'Equipment. E-quip-ment,' said John. His eyes were shut, and the breathing was so forced.

'What equipment?'

'Inside, inside coffin, meant coffin was very heavy . . . mistake . . .left it in, but funeral was then. Had to just . . . . had to just bury him.'

The breathing slowed. Emmett sat there, waiting to see if there was more. The breathing reduced again, the rasp, long and withered, came over longer periods of time now. Angela beckoned Emmett back.

'He's going,' she whispered. 'I've seen this before, too many times. This is him going. I don't think he'll be able to say much more. Let him have peace to go.'

Emmett didn't know what to do. Should he walk away? Maybe not. He stood there, his hands crossed, standing with his head slightly bowed. Angela, meanwhile, got down on her knees, reached over and held John's hand, telling him it was okay. It was all done now.

Emmett was touched by the woman's sincere care for the man. But in his head, thoughts were spinning. John had said forensics had come. They'd looked in the coffin. They'd sealed the coffin up again. And it was heavy, because they'd left equipment inside. How do you leave equipment inside checking over a body? What forensics was being done? As an undertaker, couldn't they ask? Hadn't they had time to get the court order to stop the burial? Some of these things just made little sense. Had John relayed them correctly? Was his mind accurate? He was dying, after all.

Emmett watched as Angela finally stood up. She reached up to the covers and pulled them up over John's head. She turned to Emmett.

'I'm afraid that Mr Ferguson has left us. If you don't mind, I have things to do.'

'Of course,' said Emmett. 'Thank you for your assistance. It was quite important, what was said. Did you hear any of it?'

Angela shook her head. 'You were so close in. I couldn't honestly say I did.'

That's a pity, thought Emmett. *All we have then is my word. I don't have anyone to corroborate what the man said*. He now had something to go on. He left the room and walked back down out of the care home.

Part of him thought about John lying there. The fact he would have died alone if not for Angela. Maybe it was a comfort. Emmett hoped never to find that out. He gave little thought to dying. But he liked the idea of going to sleep, maybe in the arms of a woman. But women had been few and far between, to say the least.

Maybe in the arms of a friend, he thought. For a moment, he thought about Sabine, her holding his hand as he passed on. He thought that would be a horrible thing for her to have to endure.

He trudged through the snow to his car, fired it up and looked at his watch. *Macleod is coming down. I'll meet him at the cemetery. That's the best place*, Emmett thought.

According to John Ferguson, the body had been tampered with. Something had been left in the coffin. Equipment apparently from a forensic unit operating in a way that Emmett didn't think any forensic unit would have operated. Harlow had been seen at the funeral directors even if Ferguson didn't know the name. If only he had been more awake, more with it, he could have shown a picture.

Emmett turned and drove the car down the driveway. Under his breath, he muttered, 'Godspeed, John Ferguson. And thank you.'

Chapter 21

E mmett found graveyards cold at the best of times. But in this wintry landscape, it was chilling him to the bones. And not just in a mental sense. Some people were good at outdoors. They could run around through anything. Emmett was happier inside.

He had a picture in his new house. More of a poster of a barbarian queen. One from the Northlands. All around in the picture was snow. There was a tiger, white and black, strolling beside her. The woman was dressed in attire that most people wouldn't have agreed with as the best for winter. Admittedly, they were thick winter boots, but the rest of her outfit was more like a spruced-up winter bikini. She, of course, had a massive sword and muscles that rippled. There was a large fur coat off her shoulders, but for some reason she had decided not to wrap it around her. People like that, they embrace the cold. Emmett did not. He chortled, thinking about the picture.

That was the thing about fantasy novels, especially the older ones; they were all about bronzed bodies, people that could endure any sort of hardship. Emmett was happy to be wrapped up in a large coat, hat on his head, and waterproof leggings over thermal trousers.

In front of him was the grave of Simon Matthews. He couldn't see the outline, but the headstone was there, showing where the man lay. Sabine checked in earlier, advising she had eyes on Harlow, but there wasn't a lot happening except she wasn't going to work. Instead, she was travelling around many public places and seemed to sit and think.

Emmett turned his head and he could barely make out the car that pulled into the car park, a good two hundred yards away. He recognised Macleod's car and the man getting out, who, for some reason, was still wearing a fedora hat instead of a proper winter beanie. He had a long coat on. In usual Macleod style, he strode over, never raising his head toward Emmett.

Emmett turned back and looked down at the grave.

'Why here?' asked Macleod. 'I got the text. No explanation, though. Did you just want to meet away from people?'

'This is the key here,' said Emmett. 'What lies beneath the ground there will tell us everything. I can feel it.'

'How?' asked Macleod.

'When Simon Matthews was being buried, or rather, just before that in the funeral home, Harlow was there. The undertaker at the time was a John Ferguson, who left the business years ago now. I found him in a care home. Unfortunately, he was dying, has been for several months. Nothing suspicious in it,' said Emmett.

'Are you sure?' asked Macleod. 'They can disguise things cleverly, and with an old person, much easier.'

'No, I don't think so. Anyway, he whispered some words to me about the day that Simon Matthews was buried. Apparently, a forensic team, two men, had come in and had basically said that they needed to get another look at his body. Maybe they spun him a story about evidence. He didn't go into it enough, but the man said that they had opened the coffin, had worked on the body, and then closed it up again. But in their haste, they'd left equipment behind. The men must have been in a rush. The coffin was taken, and Simon Matthews was buried. I don't know if anybody carried it, but they said just to leave the equipment inside.'

'Bit of a tale,' said Macleod.

'Forensic team, though,' said Emmett. 'What's going to happen? The guy's going to be buried. Why's the undertaker going to care? I've been told to do it by the forensic team. They've been the ones who have touched the body, not him. With the palaver that was going on around it, just get it done since Isbister was dead by then, or at least believed to have committed suicide.'

'Are you sure of that?'

'Well, actually, no. From the case notes, it's tenuous when they believe the suicide note was written, isn't it?'

'Came from the wife. Quite when she found it, it's another matter. Records aren't good,' said Macleod. 'We need to get in there. From what you're saying? Find out what was done. To the body, to the coffin.'

'That's how I see it,' said Emmett. 'But we have a problem.'

'I agree,' said Macleod. 'To get an exhumation. On what? The ramblings of a dying man which only you heard. If I had a statement, maybe that would help. Go to the sheriff with that. And given the influence of people above who want you and me off this case anyway, I don't think it'll be given.'

'No,' said Emmett. 'I'm not sure we could dig it up ourselves either.'

'No,' said Macleod. 'You've got to be careful. They want you to put a foot out of line. We do something like that, they see us doing it, we'll get thrown out. We'll never get near the case again.'

'What way do we go?' asked Emmett. He turned, walked away from the grave, and Macleod joined him. They could see the line of headstones, and Macleod hoped they were following what would have been the path underneath the snow.

'I don't know who's behind your letter,' said Emmett to Macleod. 'That's what's bugging me. Who kicks this all off? I understand that there's people who are looking to cover it up, and that's fine. Harlow knows who they are, or at least some of them. Harlow worked with them. Someone who wanted the McIntoshes taken down or had used methods that weren't right to take the McIntoshes down. I reckon that's what Matthews was finding out.'

'More than that, though,' said Macleod. 'It must have been bad enough that Matthews was prepared to work with the McIntoshes to find out about it. From what I remember of Matthews back then, and from what I've read in the reports, he's not a man who mixes with criminals, certainly not lightly. He's a truth seeker.'

'Or a pain in the arse,' said Emmett. 'Certainly, for police-public relations.'

'No organisation is ever completely clean. No organisation has people that live up to all its standards. And the police are not any different in that. And yes, in our role, we have to dig things out. But there's people who fail slightly. And there's outright deception and coercion, and going against everything that we stand for,' said Macleod. 'To simply take out the McIntoshes. Even I wouldn't have countenanced it.

'The stakes are high, however,' said Macleod. 'Donald

Mackey, according to Spanish colleagues, was killed by a professional hitman. Extreme. Apparently, the grave of Orca was dug up too. There was no cask with the ashes, Spanish authorities believe.'

'Somebody's blowing the story up then.'

'Yes,' said Macleod. 'One of the problems is that wherever you've been, things seem to have happened. Now, I know you're clean, and I know you're not instigating this, but as you said, somebody's played us. They've used us to find out who's behind this. But they haven't found out yet. Like us, they're wondering. Are things real? But unlike us, they're prepared to take action because it's their sole goal here.'

'I'm investigating a case,' said Emmett. 'But I'm still living by the rules as best I can.'

'But they've done us a favour,' said Macleod. 'It points to the fact that Harlow knew there was a cover-up. But it leaves her very exposed.'

'It does, doesn't it?' said Emmett. 'I thought it was a lie. Was convinced it was a lie the whole time. Why we were sent out there? I didn't need to prove suicide or not. And if I didn't prove it, then she was okay. At least to a point.'

'How stable is she?' asked Macleod.

'Well, you probably know her better than I did. I've only recently got to know her, in any shape, sense, or form. Even down at the station, I didn't know her. Sabine might know better. She'd have seen Sabine more than me. You know I don't fit with people. They don't like to talk to me. Everybody likes to talk to Sabine. She's friendly. She's outgoing. She's—'

'Perfect to work alongside you,' said Macleod. 'You get on well and she can pick up what you lack. That friendliness to people. But yet you've got the decisiveness. And you've got the cold mind to pull back from it. She's also a friend.'

'Some people would say that's a problem,' said Emmett.

'I haven't found that,' said Macleod. 'I worked with Hope, and at the beginning. she wasn't a friend. She was just my colleague. The more we got to know each other, saw each other's differences, the more we became friends. Friends have your back in a way that colleagues don't. Never hold her back,' said Macleod. 'But be prepared to hang on to her too.'

Emmett stared up at Macleod, but his face was impassive. Was he talking about Hope, or was he talking about Sabine? The two were so intermixed in that statement.

'There'll be a cover-up,' said Emmett. 'Another one.'

'Of course there will,' said Macleod. 'The cover's been blown out, so you've got Harlow exposed. At some point, they'll have to do something with her. These people were prepared to kill you and Sabine, admittedly out of the country, but they were prepared to do it. I don't think they'll hang about with Harlow.'

'I don't either,' said Emmett.

'When I left,' said Macleod, 'I had phone calls to my secretary asking where I was going, what I was doing. I told her to tell them I was off to Pitlochry. I told her to tell them you'd summoned me, that I'd looked excited.'

'Pushing it a bit,' said Emmett. 'When have you ever been excited?'

'That's enough,' said Macleod. 'You haven't been working with me that long. They say you have to call me Seoras. We're all on first-name terms. I think you're a good officer, Emmett. I trust you as an officer, but you don't know me well enough to make cracks like that yet.'

'No, sir,' said Emmett.

'But I'm serious. Make sure you don't overplay it. Let's take a walk back to the grave,' said Macleod, turning around to retrace his steps back.

'Why?' asked Emmett, following him.

'There's another car just pulled into the graveyard. There's a storm moving in. See the snow coming? The wind picking up? Who in their right mind would come out to visit a grave today?' said Macleod. 'Who seriously thinks that we need to visit Aunty Lily or whoever? Look at the graves. There's nothing to see today. You can't even see the ground underneath. You certainly wouldn't pitch up now with that storm about to blow in. Somebody's come looking for you and me,' said Macleod. 'And I'm going to make sure they know what we've been looking at.'

Macleod arrived at the grave of Simon Matthews and stood again, looking at it. Emmett stood beside him. For a good three or four minutes, they stood impassive while they heard someone get out of a car. The woman approached the grave about six along from Simon Matthews, placed a bunch of flowers there. She knelt down for a few moments before turning and leaving.

Macleod turned and walked after her, Emmett in full flow behind him.

'I think you dropped something,' said Macleod. The woman stopped and turned to look at him. She was wrapped up in a puffer coat, hat on top, boots below.

'What?' she asked.

Macleod pulled something from his pocket. 'Keys. Did you drop these keys?'

'Keys?' she said. The woman looked at them. 'I don't think so.'

'Oh. I'm sorry,' said Macleod. 'Just off to see your mum. I'm sorry to intrude. Really shouldn't have.'

'Yes,' said the woman. 'Mum's birthday today. I thought I'd best.'

'Sorry to disturb you,' said Macleod. 'I'll let you go.'

He turned back with Emmett, walking back towards Simon Matthews' grave. Behind them, the pair could hear the car being started and then driving off. After it did so, Macleod turned and made sure it was clear before he walked with Emmett to the grave where the woman had laid flowers.

'Us being watched then, was it? Where did you get those keys?' asked Emmett.

'The keys are mine. However, unless her mother had a sex change in life, she wasn't here to visit that grave.'

Emmett turned and looked at the stone. 'The birth date's wrong too. Not her birthday, is it?'

'No,' said Macleod. 'But she saw who we were looking at. Cat's amongst the pigeons now with what's happened in Spain. You wait and see.'

He reached down suddenly and pulled his phone out. He held a hand up to Emmett.

'Really? I don't think that's right,' said Macleod. 'From above? I appreciate it, Jim. Understand where you're coming from. No, it is wrong. It's absolutely wrong. I'm not happy about it. I'll put a formal complaint in about it. It's my department. I should have a right to send them where I want. It's cold cases. Okay, it's not strictly a cold case in that sense, Jim. You're right. Okay. I'll deal with it, okay? I appreciate the funding was for that, and it wasn't for—but that's an injustice, or at least a lack of justice being administered properly,' said Macleod.

He was grinning at Emmett. 'I'll get it sorted. You know you can trust me, Jim. I'm on it. Okay.'

Macleod closed down the phone call and put the phone back in his pocket.

'Well, well, well,' he said. 'That was the ACC telling me you need to get your backside off to Inverness and get into the case pile sitting in the cold case office. You don't want to be here because the Spanish incident looks like it's going to get out of control. You need to be reined in.'

'Do you think the ACC's involved in this?'

'Jim's not involved,' said Macleod. 'He's a lot of things, but at heart, he's a decent copper and he wouldn't go to these lengths. He likes things to go smoothly. He sometimes sees things the wrong way and has to be told. But he's not a bad policeman. He's not corrupt. He's had pressure from above. Well done, Emmett,' said Macleod.

'Thank you,' said Emmett. 'I think.'

'You've chucked a stone in the water. The ripples are on the move, and the boats are starting to toss and turn. So much so that they're about to make for a safer harbour, and they don't care who they leave in the water behind to get there. There's no way we're heading back north. Not when all the action's about to kick off,' said Macleod. 'Come on. It's been at least an hour since I had a coffee.'

Chapter 22

S abine Ferguson was a little perturbed. She'd been tailing DCI Harlow for most of the day. The woman had gone from coffee shop to restaurant to coffee shop. Busy ones. Establishments in shopping centres. Places that had plenty of people about. Motorway services. Everywhere she was, there were lots of people.

Sabine was sure she'd been clocked and not just once. Several times. It wasn't that easy remaining incognito, considering the places that Harlow had gone. But the thing that bothered Sabine was that Harlow didn't seem to want to get away from her. In fact, she was almost making it obvious to Sabine where she was. At one point, Sabine was sure Harlow had waited for her.

However, Harlow hadn't met with anyone. In fact, the other thing she noticed was that even when she went to the toilet, she never went to an empty one. There was a nervousness about the woman, too. But not when she was looking at Sabine. No, she wasn't bothered about Sabine. The nervousness came when she was looking beyond Sabine at other faces.

Right now, she was sitting in a shopping centre cafe at the front, just outside the shop, at a small table. There was a cordoned off area with several tables in it, and they were full at the moment. Harlow was sitting at one table, a coffee in front of her, and Sabine wasn't sure she'd touched it.

Sabine was getting dirty looks from the bookstore owner who's shop she was standing in. She'd been there for over twenty minutes, and she'd barely looked at the books, glancing at the occasional one.

Sabine saw the bookshop owner was coming over towards her as she closed another book, put it back on the shelf and picked up a separate one.

He came up close and then whispered in her ear.

'Excuse me, madam. There are things called libraries, and you're more than welcome to go there and stand and read. Quite happy for people to browse what they want, but most people end up buying a book, not simply reading them.'

Sabine hadn't read a word, but she couldn't really say that to him, could she? Don't worry about me. I'm watching someone else.

'Sorry,' said Sabine, 'I'm just interested in this book.' She looked down at it, not having just grabbed it.

"Living with Male Prostate Cancer," said the man. 'That's interesting, because the book before that was on breastfeeding. The one before that,' he said, 'was about mumps and children. You've been through the entire medical section here. Some sort of trainee doctor, pet?'

Sabine nearly burst out laughing. She hadn't even caught what she was reading. She turned round for a moment to the man. 'I'm sorry,' she said, and opened her jacket slightly, reaching inside to pull out her warrant card. She kept it hidden from most other people, covered over by her jacket, but the bookshop owner could see.

'I'll get on the move,' she said. 'I'm watching someone. So, apologies for wasting your time.'

'Maybe you could work on your cover,' said the man. 'Either that or you could dress to fit the books.'

Sabine's mind suddenly raced to what someone who was reading these three books would actually look like. It took only a moment to realise it would be a world of trouble in today's political climate to even begin to describe that person. She instead smiled, put the warrant card away, and left the shop.

As she did so, she saw Harlow looking at her. The woman was waving her over. Well and truly clocked, Sabine decided now was the time to bite the bullet, and she walked over and inside the cordon, where the table was located.

'I don't think my budget's going to cover much more coffee. Why don't you get one for the both of us? I won't move,' said Harlow. 'Probably worth a chat.'

Sabine nodded, looked at the cold coffee in front of Harlow, and guessed it was a latte. She disappeared inside the shop but watched the table. Harlow didn't move. Returning with two coffees, she placed one in front of Harlow.

'I don't know if you take sugar, sweetener, or whatever.'

'It's fine,' Harlow said, and Sabine sat down opposite her.

'You need to get better at following people,' said Harlow. 'Though in truth I was expecting you. There's been a right ruckus out in Spain.'

'I haven't heard,' said Ferguson.

'Well, somebody went and dug up a grave. Wasn't you, was it?'

'No, I've been back to the UK for a while now. Wasn't worth us digging up the grave, bringing the Spanish authorities to make it happen. Somebody, however, killed Dr Perez.'

Harlow nodded. 'Yes, unfortunate. Trouble was, the man did little else. That's the thing when you work for people. If you just do one thing, and then covers are going to get blown, you're not that useful to them. If you've done more than one thing, if you've done several things, well, then they're more likely to keep you alive.'

'Is that what you've done?'

Harlow took a sip of her coffee and placed it down.

'I've done plenty,' she said. 'Much more than you'll ever know. That's the thing, you see,' said Harlow. 'You don't understand the depths to which these things run. You come in as a young officer, and you do well. And you've done well around Glasgow. Very well. You're impressive.'

'Well, forgive me if I don't start returning compliments,' said Sabine. 'When you tell me what you've been doing, and you've done a lot, it doesn't mean that much to me.'

'There's no need to be like that,' said Harlow. 'Look at you. Six-foot, black hair, trim. Not stupid either. Good in the arts world, I heard. Must have been. You worked for Clarissa Urquhart, and she actually trusted you with arts. That woman trusts no one on the arts side. They really have to know their stuff. You should have stayed there. It's not the same type of world. Bit of elegance to it, too. You wouldn't have been a threat to anyone over there. People would have quite happily have let you get on with it. And the other departments, the other ones, they'd have looked at you and thought that's the type of woman we want around. Young, sexy.'

'I don't think I want to be somebody's pretty little girl stuck away in an arts department,' said Sabine.

'No, you don't, do you? You want to be the one clearing it

up, running around, getting your hands dirty and sorting out the world. I was like that once. Didn't stay like it, though, for long. You make a compromise. Maybe you're lucky. Maybe you've picked the right person to attach yourself to.'

'What do you mean by that?'

'Grump,' said Harlow. 'My God, you attached yourself to Grump. The man's bizarre. I remember going past your arts office, seeing all his little figures that he painted. Still, I guess it's better than a load of porno mags thrown around. Gambling, drinking, some of the other vices some others are into. He must be a weird sort, though.'

Sabine didn't take the bait. Everybody said stuff about him. Grump was not the standard police officer. He had some different hobbies. Wholesome. Strange in some ways, but wholesome. Sabine knew they were fun. And yes, they certainly weren't drinking, gambling, doing drugs, or pushing prostitution. But then again, there weren't a lot of officers that went into those things. A lot of officers were just sports people or good family types.

'Did you get into the wrong sort?' asked Sabine. 'Did you follow the wrong star?'

'I did. I was quite the girl back in the day, but enjoyed it. You know? Men wanting you. It's funny, isn't it? They always talk about them coming after us. But there were plenty of us going after them, too. And I hooked a good few. I moved up the ranks but a couple of them, a couple of them were well shady. And I got involved, did a few things for them, covered a few things up. Once you start, well, you don't stop. And you're wise not to stop. Because Dr Perez had one job, one secret he was keeping. Well, when that secret was blown, or rather it looked like it was about to be blown, something he could give away easily, they took him out. But if you know lots of secrets, and you're wise, and you've got the secrets in a place that will leak afterwards, well, you can keep them at bay.' She looked wistfully off now, into the supermarket.

'You could come and just tell us.'

'You are so young,' said Harlow suddenly. 'No idea how brutal these things can be.'

'You tried to shoot me in Spain.'

Harlow raised her eyebrows for a moment and then shrugged her shoulders. 'Out of the UK, more difficult to investigate, get a foreigner to do it. Never get traced back, never be worked out why you were killed. Wouldn't have been my move, though. Don't mess about with police officers. Not until you have to. Not until something's big enough to cover up.'

'Something was big enough with Orca, was it?'

Harlow laughed, but it was hollow. 'You don't get it, do you? You spend your life running around for these people, these higher powers. Not just your DCI, not just your ACC, but people above that. They're not even in the force, people that move things, people that make things happen in a big way, with real money, real influence. You do it for them, and for the rest of your life, you just run around clearing up their shit.

'That's what I've done. And if you don't, you're gone. They want to know that they can trust you to wipe up their mess. They're like babies, really. Hopefully, you've got a nappy on them. But if you don't, the poo's everywhere, and you have to clean it up. They'll even wee on you if you don't sort things out in time.'

Sabine wasn't quite sure that the comparison worked, but she was getting the idea. 'You've just gone from cup of coffee to cup of coffee today. Eaten, drunk, but won't they miss you at the office.'

'I'll go to the office. I won't get there until the end of the day, but I can't just vanish either. Cos, they'll come. They'll check the ports. I've got to do it right. I'm getting out, you see. Don't think about stopping me from here. Don't grab me. Don't arrest me. I'll be dead before you can get a word out of me.

'But I want to get away, and I want to know that you won't come after me. I don't fear them. I can go where they won't find me. But they brought Macleod into it. It's funny, isn't it? He used to call Clarissa Urquhart his Rottweiler. Oh, and she's a bitch. She's a bitch when she gets hold of you. But she is nothing on the old man himself.

'All these years, and he's come after this one. All these years, and he's launched you and Grump straight into this. Nothing subtle about it, was there? Absolutely nothing. I tried to waylay, I tried to give the option, but no. And now he's down, down to Pitlochry, standing over the grave of Simon Matthews. He was not letting it go, and he won't let it go, ever. I heard once—and you can tell me if this is true—he actually followed someone on their holiday, because he couldn't convict them, but he knew they'd done it. Or is that just rumour?'

'I don't know him that well,' said Sabine. 'But yes, he's tenacious.'

'Tenacious,' said Harlow. 'He's not tenacious. He's a man who doesn't know life outside of work. Seen too many of them. But I will have a life outside of work. I've got money stashed away. Made them pay me. I made them give me rewards for what I did. But Macleod will.

'Tell him I want to meet him. Tell him I want to give him

everything that he needs to get after those higher up. He won't be able to resist cleaning up the force. It's the one thing he hates. Bent coppers and those higher up. I'll give him all the evidence. I'll show him where it is. And all he's got to do is let me run. Not come after me. He's got to keep them busy for so long that they forget about me.'

Sabine drank some of her coffee, watching Harlow. The woman put the mug down, having finished her latte. 'I'll be in contact with him,' she said. 'He can tell me yes or no. I don't think anyone's following me at the moment, so I'm going to disappear. I'll give him a place to meet me. We'll go. I'll give him the evidence. Hard evidence. Paperwork, everything he needs. It'll take an hour or two. And then he leaves. Does what he needs to do. And he won't see me ever again.

'That's the deal. And it's the only deal he'll get. He arrests me, I'm dead. He lets me go and tries to come after me elsewhere, they'll follow him. They'll tail him and I'll be dead before he gets his evidence. This is a one off. I have a place. I know where to go. A couple of hours, gone. Go tell him that.'

'I will,' said Sabine. 'Do you have his number?'

'I do and I'll call him,' Harlow glanced at her watch. 'Will call him tonight. Eight o'clock. It won't be from my phone, though. That's gone.'

Harlow stood up and almost seemed to smile, like a weight was dropping off her shoulders.

'I had a lot of thinking to do today,' she said to Sabine. 'You should think well, too. You're a good-looking lass. I'm sure there's plenty you could do in life. Don't get hauled in with the likes of Macleod. Chasing up horror stories, cases that nobody wants solved because it stirs up too much shit. Investigate something you can win at. Something that when you go home at night, you just sleep. You're not worried about what else has gone on? Stay out of the real dark stuff. It's about your life. It's not about the rubbish. Go have a good one instead.'

She went to walk off, but Sabine told her to wait. 'Grump says that if you don't clear up the mess, clear up the dark, it grows and grows and it gets bigger and it overcomes. And everything that's worth saving in life goes. He says the heroes are the ones that stand against the darkness. The heroes are the ones that stand in the light.'

'You do that, you'll end up a corpse and an unhappy one. I'll take it he's into making speeches, your Grump.'

Sabine smiled as Harlow walked away. Emmett had actually said it, introducing a new game, which Sabine was going to be playing a character in. It was funny, as it was the only time he ever tried to be melodramatic. It just didn't quite work. But she realised that for all the games he played, all Emmett was looking for was a better world and how to do it.

Chapter 23

Macleod sat in the passenger seat of the car with Emmett beside him. Emmett was getting through a burger and chips, but Macleod wasn't hungry. He had taken a coffee as they both waited for Sabine to join them. The car, however, was getting cold and Macleod wrapped his coat round him as best he could.

That was the trouble at his age. Things never felt good.

'And she just said she needed to see us? Had left the target? Just let Harlow go?'

'Trust her,' said Emmett. 'Sabine's not daft. You've worked with her before.'

'But Harlow could be gone. Harlow could go to ground.'

'Sabine will have her reasons. Says she needs to meet you, so she must want to talk about it, and face to face.'

Macleod could barely see out of the windows of the car. Now they were parked, the snow had fallen hard, and Emmett hadn't turned on the engine to start the wipers again. It was a shock then when the rear door opened, and Sabine jumped in.

'Flipping cold out there,' she said.

'On the seat beside you,' said Emmett. Sabine looked over and there was a wrapped-up burger and chips. 'I'm not sure if the chips will be warm anymore.'

Sabine gave Emmett a smile. That's where the friend was, not the boss. Macleod, however, was staring at Sabine.

'So what is it?' asked Macleod.

Sabine reached over, grabbed the chips, and started woofing some into her mouth.

'What is it, Ferguson?' said Macleod. Sabine stared back.

'You haven't used Ferguson in a long time. It's not what you do anymore.' He was obviously edgy. 'Thing is,' she said, mumbling through the chips.

'Stop and eat them and then say,' said Emmett.

'Just say,' blurted Macleod.

Sabine swallowed the chips that were in her mouth quickly and then said, 'Harlow is going to go on the run. She said she wants to meet you. And when she meets you, she'll give you all the evidence you need to go at all the people up above her, everything that's happened, and then she'll run. She says she's got somewhere to go, she's got the money, and she will disappear.'

'What? Give me the evidence? Why tell you this?' asked Macleod.

'She said that she's basically had to clean up their shit all her life.' Sabine saw Macleod raise his eyebrows at the language and she said, 'That the one thing she was worried about was you. She said that Clarissa was nothing of a Rottweiler compared to you. That your teeth were into this. That you were still coming at this after all these years.'

'She won't know, will she?' said Emmett. 'She won't know that you were prompted into it.'

'No, she won't,' said Macleod. 'She is really that scared that I'll come after her?'

190

'She seemed to be. She was angry too. Angry at those she was working for. Told me how she started off. Fun and simple, but once you've done something, you have to keep going. Otherwise, you end up like Dr Perez.'

'There is a sense in that,' said Macleod. 'I get it. The more you have, the more you can tell, up to a point. They will eventually get rid of you, anyway. But they'll take their time, because they'll have to find out where you store the things you know about them. Where you are going to pass it on. Leverage is only leverage until it's gone. Whether you have used it, or whether they take it off you,' said Macleod. 'She must be pretty confident she thinks she can hide from them.'

'She thinks they'll be so busy with you chasing after them and dumping them in so much trouble, that they won't even have time to go after her.'

Macleod turned and sat back, looking forward.

'I'm not so sure about that,' said Emmett. 'Really? She really thinks she can run?'

'People sometimes get cocky,' said Macleod. 'Happens to people who've been doing things for a long time. You forget your vulnerability. Forget how dangerous the people are you're up against.'

'You think she's genuine?' Emmett said to Sabine.

'I don't know,' said Sabine, unwrapping the burger. 'I really don't. She sat there all day, looking for somebody, looking for people, and then she turned round and just waved me over.'

'She look frightened?' asked Emmett.

'She did. All day she looked frightened. Stayed very public. She was watching people all the time. She didn't look bothered when she saw me. In fact, Harlow looked glad I was there.'

'It's a risk,' said Macleod.

'It's a risk you've got until eight o'clock to decide,' said Sabine. 'She'll call you at eight o'clock. She'll give you somewhere to go. You go there. She spends an hour or two with you, gives you all the evidence to take away. You drive away. She goes her own way. You never meet again, and you go hook, line, and sinker after these other ones.'

'Very neat,' said Macleod.

'So what are you thinking?' asking Sabine. 'Should we do it?'

'Well, think about it,' said Macleod. 'From one side, it makes sense. It's what we initiated. Emmett and I stood over the grave of Simon Matthews. They know we want to get into it. They know he's been to see the old undertaker. We know there were shenanigans around the coffin. They know we know that. They think we're onto this, in a big way. So very soon, I think, they'll act. And they would act by taking her out for a start. She must know that, too. So from that point of view, it makes sense. However, the one thing they've done all along is play us.'

'So,' said Emmett, 'what are you thinking?'

'The prize is big enough. It's worth the risk,' said Macleod.

'She wants you alone,' said Sabine.

'I'll go alone, because if she gets wind of anybody else there, she thinks she's being captured and then she'll run. And we'll not get the evidence. She'll do something else with it. It'll be me on my own. We treat it as genuine. We do it as genuine. Because if we don't, we won't get the evidence. It's a risk worth taking,' said Macleod.

'It's a big risk,' said Sabine. 'Very big risk. No backup. No one to get you out.'

'Seoras,' said Emmett. 'You're not the fittest.'

'I'd do all right for my age,' said Macleod.

'Put Sabine in there,' said Emmett. 'She'll probably get out. But even that would be risky. Take your Kirsten Stewart, put her in there, no problem. Wouldn't be that worried—knows what to look for. But this, this is something; if we get it wrong, you're going to struggle to walk back out of. You go in cold, with no backup and it won't work if she's lying to you. Too much of a risk.'

'That's my call,' said Macleod. 'It's me that's being put under threat, so it's my call. And I'm running the department, in case you've forgotten, Emmett.'

Sabine also had a worried face in the rear of the car.

'Sometimes,' said Emmett, 'people get so long in their work that they think themselves impervious to danger. They can come through anything, get it wrong once, and they don't have to think about it again.'

'Are you questioning my judgment?' asked Macleod.

'Massively,' said Emmett. 'Your life is not worth this.'

'What she's offering,' said Macleod, 'is taking down a cancer, a corruption within our ranks. For the good of every decent officer out there, of course, it's worth it.'

'I'm with Emmett,' said Sabine.

'Well, I'm afraid I overruled you. Eight o'clock, you say,' said Macleod.

'Eight o'clock,' said Sabine.

Silence filled the car.

* * *

At eight o'clock, Macleod was sitting in a lay-by with Emmett and Sabine sat behind him in another car. The pair watched him as he took a phone call, precisely on eight. He quickly closed the call, got out of his car, and walked back to where Emmett rolled down the window.

'I'm to go to Stirling Services,' he said. 'She'll direct me from there. You two remain here. I've got my phone, I can phone you if needs be.'

'She'll not let you have the phone on,' said Emmett. 'She'll make you drop it, make you put it somewhere else. That's why we're on the move here.'

'Possibly,' said Macleod. 'Decision's made. Stay here, I'll get in contact.'

He walked off and Emmett gripped the steering wheel of the car, his knuckles going white due to the tightness of his grip.

'It is his choice,' said Sabine.

'Don't like it,' said Emmett. 'They've led us down the garden path the whole way.'

'You think she's not being genuine?'

'More than that,' said Emmett. 'Think about it. From somebody high up's perspective. You've got Harlow. She's a problem,' he said. 'You've got Macleod. Big problem. How do you kill off both of your problems? How do you stop them from becoming an issue?'

'Well, you could take out a contract. Just kill her. Kill him. If you killed her, Macleod wouldn't have much to go on,' said Sabine.

'And that would stop him? You kill her, and he's a problem. He will dig like anything because you just said to him she had stuff, she had major stuff, so much we got rid of her,' said Emmett, incredibly animated.

'So what?' said Sabine.

'You tell her you're going to close him down. You use her

to get him somewhere to close him down. That leaves her vulnerable. She's going to take him to somewhere off the grid, away from everybody. Handing over evidence, that's what she's saying to him. She won't want anybody there, won't want any proof that it happened. Perfect. He's then gone somewhere, probably phoneless, with nobody else coming to check up on him. She'll get there, thinking she's hauling him in to be taken out and, lo-and-behold, they come along and they take out the pair of them.'

'You're right,' said Sabine. 'That's a play. They could make that play. If she's not being genuine, they could make that play. It fits.'

'He knows it, too,' said Emmett.

'What?' said Sabine. 'He will not walk into that if he knows that.'

'Of course he knows it,' said Emmett. 'He's going off your judgment. He's put his whole life on what you saw with Harlow,' said Emmett.

Sabine shifted uncomfortably. 'But I said I didn't know. I said I was unsure. I said, yes, she looked like she was frightened. Yes, she looked—'

'He thinks he can work it, thinks he'll get out of it. He thinks he's good enough when there's trouble.'

'You don't?' said Sabine.

'No,' said Emmett. He reached down underneath his seat and pulled up a device. It had a screen that was currently showing a map. There was a dot on the map that was on the move. 'That's the DCI. He's arrived at Stirling Services,' said Emmett.

About thirty seconds later, a text arrived. Macleod advised he was to go to a cottage, but he was leaving his phone behind. He didn't give where the cottage was. He said he was standing in front of a camera and placing the phone in front of the camera, giving only the text to tell everybody to stand down and stay away.

Emmett watched the screen along with Sabine as Macleod travelled, just over a mile from Stirling Services, the dot was showing a field and a building. Emmett got on the move. As they drove up towards the services and past it, heading further north, Emmett pulled away and parked up a half a kilometre away. Rather than parking in a lay-by, Emmett drove the car down the side of the lay-by, leaving it just over the side.

'It's over there,' said Sabine. 'Right over there.'

The night was dark, snow whipping round and round. They dressed in black, scarves wrapped around their faces, beanie hats on, with fleeces underneath waterproofs.

'Let's go,' said Emmett.

Together, they marched through a field, heading towards the cottage which sat in the middle of nowhere. There was a river running across the fields, and Sabine told Emmett to follow her down. They walked along the bank, before stepping down into the river itself.

Emmett could feel the water, halfway up his shin. Then, as they moved along as quickly as possible, his bones were frozen.

'Keep going,' said Sabine. 'It's the only way to keep warm. They won't hear us with the noise of the river, either.'

Walking on, Sabine stopped, believing they'd arrived as close to the cottage as the river allowed. Sabine and Emmett walked up the bank and lay down just at the top of it so they could see the cottage that Macleod had driven to.

There were two cars outside, his and Harlow's. Inside, lights were on. But as they stood watching, Sabine could see another car arriving.

'That one. Look at that one, that's coming down the track,' said Sabine.

Emmett pulled binoculars from out of his jacket. He took a careful look. 'Black limo,' he said.

'Black limo? You mean like the one that was there before?'

'Yes,' said Emmett. 'Exactly like the one she met before.'

Chapter 24

Macleod stood in what was a disused room. Drab wallpaper, patterned like something he remembered from the 80s, was peeling down off the walls. There was a sofa, but he thought he wouldn't bother with it because of the rips.

The windows in the room were fragile, to say the least, and you could hear the wind whistling at them. One room they'd come through had a large bay window, which was the noisiest. The cottage had a central hallway leading off to different rooms, which also had connections to the surrounding rooms. Harlow had taken him around them all, checking doors, making sure everything was locked to the outside before she came into this room.

There was a small table, a trestle that had been opened out, on the top of which sat several manila envelopes filled to the brim with papers. Harlow now stood beside them.

'You know the deal,' she said. 'Before we start, I want you to tell me you'll get away, that you won't come after me.'

'If what you say is true, if there's enough evidence there, to go after all these people that you say you work for, I won't,' said Macleod. 'You have my word on that.'

'It's very trusting of you,' she said, 'but I'll run through it with you for the next hour or so. Do you want some coffee first? I know you're a coffee man but I'm not daft. I didn't bring instant. The flask has got some real coffee in it. Why don't you pour us some?'

Macleod looked over to another table set against the wall. On it was a large flask and two mugs.

'I didn't bring any milk, but you like it black, don't you? I seem to remember that from the station. Back in the good old days. Do you remember them, Macleod?'

Macleod raised his eyebrows, but then walked over, opened the flask, and smelt the pleasing aroma of coffee. He poured a cup for himself, one for Harlow, and then carried them both over towards her before handing one across.

'You could have just sent this by file transfer,' said Macleod.

'Oh no,' said Harlow. 'It would be traced. We can't have them tracing me.'

'It's not for me,' said Macleod. 'I don't understand how it all works.'

'This stuff is what we grew up with. We had filing systems back then. You just put bits of paper into the correct folder. Computers were only getting going. Like when we started. You remember those days, do you, Macleod? Simpler times, I thought.'

'I don't think things have changed,' said Macleod. 'People are just people, whatever the time they live in. Those that try to live right, those who decide not to. Those who decide to take more off everyone else and don't care how they get it.'

Harlow sipped her coffee and then stared at him. 'Well, what's it got you? You were a miserable bugger back then. Miserable. Hard to flippin' work with. They dumped Isbister with you. You realise that, don't you? The Orcadian. Another one from the islands. Strange people you guys were. Strange.'

'Can we get down to it?' asked Macleod. 'I wouldn't have thought you'd want to be here that long.'

'Of course,' she said. 'It's all there. You can start looking through it.'

Macleod reached down and picked up the first manila envelope. He pulled the flap back and saw a blank piece of paper on top. He took it out. Inside were all different pages of paper, but all were blank.

'What's this?' he asked.

'Oh, there's more there,' said Harlow.

Macleod picked up the next one. It was full of blank pieces of paper as well, which he let drop on the floor. Inside, his stomach got tight. He stepped forward, but Harlow put her hands up, one still holding the coffee.

'You can frisk me if you want. I have no weapons,' she said. 'Wouldn't trust myself to do that. I was surprised you fell for it. No phone, nothing. Just you here. A good man too, so I'm safe enough.'

Even though the wind was blowing outside, Macleod could now hear a car engine. He tore over to the window. Looking out, he saw a black limousine. He turned back to Harlow.

'They didn't ask you to do it,' he said.

'No. Sending over one of their own. Specialist. I won't know who they are, but they'll be here to do it.'

'They sent someone here to kill an unarmed man when you're here. When you've set it up. When you've—'

'Yes,' said Harlow, almost defiantly. 'That's it exactly. I reeled you in for them. They'll dispose of you, and I'll continue. Things will be sorted out from above. Sure, I might have to be off to the doctor for a bit. But Mr Matthews will never come out of that grave that you were looking to get into. It will remain undisturbed. The secrets will remain safe. I'd tell you who they are, but frankly, we haven't time. You see, I locked all the doors so you wouldn't get out. But he's got a key. The man that's coming.'

Macleod heard a key turn in the lock out in the hallway.

'Are you that stupid?' asked Macleod. 'They would get you to do it. Would get you to do it so you would be implicated in it. They don't just get you to set it up. They make you do it. Then, you won't talk about it. Because at the moment, all you've done is invite me here. If you kill me, you're banged to rights. But now you're to witness it. It means they're not just coming for me. They're closing the whole loop down, making sure nobody can speak about it. They're coming for you too, Harlow. And you've gone and told me you're unarmed.'

Macleod saw the realisation on the woman's face. She was going white now, panicking. But Macleod tore over to where the coffee had sat and moved the table across to one door of the room. There were three doors, in and out. It was a cottage, yes, with a central hallway. Rooms were lined off either side, six in total. But each room could go into the other, be it the kitchen at the rear, the two bedrooms, the living room, the dining room, or the utility room. At least that's what Macleod called them, for there wasn't much furniture to give their former identities away.

The front door closed. Macleod turned, looked to the door behind him, opened it, and stepped through into the kitchen at the rear of the cottage. *What way to play this*, he thought. *What way?* But already Harlow was with him.

'There's two of us,' she said. 'Two of us we can take him.'

Macleod looked at her. The thing they always said about older detectives was that the brain was still functioning. The brain was quick; it was clever. What they never said about older detectives was 'Oh, and if we get somebody big and physical in, those guys will take them.' That's why Macleod always had younger people about and people who could be physical when needed. It was important, especially when you weren't, at least not anymore.

Macleod heard another door open, but it never shut. He stepped out of the kitchen, peering into the hallway, and then stepped through another door into the utility room at the rear. It was white, or at least had been once before the light had turned it to a stained yellow. There were pipes there that would have held the outlet for a washing machine, but there were no appliances there.

Macleod held his finger up to his mouth, showing Harlow should be quiet. Could he sneak past? Could they get out the front door? If they did, it wouldn't matter because the limo was there.

* * *

'That man's just gone in with a gun,' said Sabine. 'They're off to execute him. We need to go.'

Emmett didn't have time to agree because Sabine was away. She took a line that went behind the limousine that had arrived. And as she got closer, one of the limo doors opened. A man stepped out with a gun. She hit him, full bore with her shoulder in the midriff, carrying him into the car door that he'd just opened. She heard the cry. and was up and on her feet again in no time, racing for the house.

Behind her, Emmett was a little slower, but he was getting going. A man had stepped out from the passenger side at the front of the car and had been taken down by Sabine. Now someone was stepping out of the driver's side. He was bringing a gun up to bear, ready to fire it.

Emmett ran as quick as he could to intercept the man, but he would not make it in time. He reached down with his gloved hands, scooping up a large pile of the snow, and compacted it tightly within his hands. He continued, but drew back the snowball he'd created in his hands, and threw it as hard as he could towards the driver.

The gun was being steadied, resting across the other arm, ready to shoot, when the snowball smacked the man on the side of the head. A shot, silenced, went askew, and the man turned to see who had hit him, slightly baffled. By the time he did, Emmett had reached the car door and pushed it hard with all his might, squeezing the man, trapping him between the door and the car. The man grunted, and the gun fell from his hand.

Emmett drove his elbow at the man's head, hitting him robustly, but the man then pushed the door back, sending Emmett sprawling on the ground. The gun was somewhere between the two of them and the man, still wheezing, pushed the door forward and stepped to one side. He went to make a jump for the gun while Emmett had only just got back to his feet. The man clearly was going to win.

Emmett ran forward and, seeing the man's head coming down beside the gun with the hand reaching forward, Emmett kicked the head for all he was worth.

He imagined it being like a penalty, foot beside the ball, strike it as clean and as hard as you could. The man grunted and toppled away. Emmett reached down and flung the gun as far as he could. Circling the car, Emmett saw the gun of the passenger, who was still lying on the ground wheezing. He grabbed the man's gun, flinging it as far away as he could.

Emmett made for the house.

* * *

Macleod stepped out into the hall. If the gunman was coming down one side, Macleod was banking on the premise they would loop around the outside room to room. He doubted his pursuer would route through the hallway. There was a commotion building outside, so Macleod made a run for it up that central passage.

Halfway along, as he went past the lounge he'd been in before, its door opened and Macleod was shoved hard against the door opposite. The door wasn't locked; it swung open, and Macleod tumbled into one of the other rooms. It was the sitting room with a large bay window, and he could hear the wind howling through it.

But he was more concerned about a gunman who now had grabbed Harlow. She'd followed Macleod and was thrown into the room as well. Macleod backed away as best he could towards the wall. The gunman kicked Harlow on the ground in front of him and then turned to look at Macleod.

'Not so fast, Inspector. Don't you leave.'

The man was wearing a balaclava. He turned now, back to Harlow. She was white, scrabbling towards the wall.

'They said I had to say this to you beforehand. You failed them. One must deal with things yourself. You're employed by them. Not to come running, crying to us when things go wrong. You let them get in too deep. They know. They know about the grave. So now you say we have to kill him as well. You brought that about. You failed.'

Macleod jumped as the gun fired. There was no loud retort, but he watched as the bullet pierced the front of her head and blood spattered on her face and on the wall behind. A second shot followed almost instantly.

'And now your turn, Inspector.'

Macleod put a hand up, but he could still hear noise from outside. The gunman looked that way, too.

'Let me stand,' said Macleod. 'I'm not dying like this. I'll turn and you can walk behind me. Quick and close.'

'They said we owed you that. Decent but nosey copper. Fine, up you get. Be quick.'

Macleod went to get up, then feigned to fall back down again. The gunman came over and put an arm under Macleod's shoulder. The man was strong, lifting Macleod to his feet.

As they were halfway up to standing, Macleod heard one, two, three thuds. The hand of the gunman was whipped away from under Macleod's arm. It was difficult to perceive what then happened. Afterwards, Sabine would tell him she had turned into the room, seen the gunman lifting Macleod up, and had gone for him full pelt.

She had lowered her shoulder, caught him in under the ribs, and driven him hard towards the window. It was in such a fragile state. The pane collapsed, and the pair had tumbled outside into the snow, glass breaking around them.

Sabine rolled after she'd hit the ground. She felt glass cutting the side of her face. The gunman was rising too with the gun lying in the snow close to him. He would beat her to it, and not by a short margin. He realised this too, and quickly he staggered as best he could to the gun.

From the window, where the glass had broken out behind him, Sabine now saw a figure put a foot up onto the sill and jump. The figure landed on top of the gunman, knocking him back to the ground. It was Emmett, and he came down hard, letting go a cry as he hit the ground.

Sabine ran for the gun, picking it up just as the gunman had got back up. He grabbed hold of her other arm. He was holding her right hand, where she had the gun with the left. It wasn't her good hand. She was right-handed, would aim that way, and she felt him pull her towards him. She flung the gun with everything she had. The gunman threw a punch up to her face, knocking her backwards, almost blacking her out, and she thudded into the ground. The snow piled up around her head.

'Get out of here. We need to get out of here,' shouted a voice.

Sabine saw Macleod jumping through the window and Emmett getting back to his feet, clutching his sore ribs. The gunman took a quick look at them and then ran.

Macleod staggered around the end of the house, and Sabine saw him reach down into his pocket. There was no phone, and he turned round, shouting at Emmett for his. Macleod came over, grabbed Emmett's phone and dialled.

Sabine lay back in the snow, the breath knocked out of her, pain in her head, ringing after the punch. And then someone collapsed on top of her. She felt arms linking around under her neck, pulling her close.

'You good?' said Emmett breathlessly. 'Are you good?'

'Yes,' said Sabine. 'I'm all right. I'm sore, but I'm all right.'

Emmett sat back up off her. And he saw the blood across her face.

'You're bleeding,' he said. But he shook his head. 'You are. Not too bad, though. Not too bad.'

Chapter 25

I t was three weeks later, and Macleod was back in Pitlochry. He stood over the re-buried Simon Matthews. After the incident at the cottage, and with Harlow now dead, people from higher up had got involved. Macleod had explained what had happened and had detailed through all the investigations that should follow.

Harlow had been identified as being shot and killed in the house, exactly as Macleod had described. The house, however, gave up no other clues. The paper that was blank had remained, but the limo had gone with the three men. They'd all been masked, so descriptions were vague—you certainly couldn't convict anybody based on just their height.

Sabine had needed a couple of stitches, the cut on her face being nasty if not particularly life-threatening. Emmett had simply bruised some of his ribs, but Macleod was impressed by how he'd reacted. The man was selfless, determined, and he reminded him of Perry, throwing themselves out there even if they weren't the most agile or determined of people.

Macleod had forced the issue around the grave, and nobody could stop it being exhumed this time. When they had done, they'd found two bodies. The second one was subsequently identified as Gavin Isbister. He had been reburied two days before the current funeral, and Macleod had stood watching his old colleague going into the ground. Gavin's wife, Isabelle, had been there with her new husband. The man kept an eye on everything, watching whatever was done. Macleod had gone to speak to her, but the man had moved in.

Macleod wasn't to be speaking to her, it seemed, though he wasn't sure whose decision that was. She seemed genuine in the tears shed as they lowered Gavin's now-long-deceased body into the grave. Harlow had a police funeral three days before that which they'd all attended. Macleod hadn't been that bothered about going. He barely knew her and yes, maybe it was something you did, but he didn't think she deserved it.

Although the snow was now gone, the wind was still cold. Macleod stood beside Emmett and Sabine saying very little. The public and the other mourners had drifted away, but Macleod had remained, determined to think things through. The ACC had come down, but even he was disappearing off back up to Inverness.

'I think this is the end of the line,' said Macleod.

'How?' asked Emmett. 'There's a level of corruption higher up.'

'Maybe,' said Macleod. 'But they've made sure that nobody knows how to get at it. Harlow would have known the next link up, at least. She's dead. Donald Mackey's dead. Dr Perez is dead. Sometimes you have to know when to let go.'

'How do you mean?' asked Sabine.

'Well, back when it all happened, I couldn't do anything. I didn't have the ability to get stuck into it. I didn't have knowledge of the people involved. When the letter came, I knew something was up. I knew something was different. And now I had the power and the clout to put somebody onto it.'

'You've not got any power and clout to do anything about it now? You can't push the ACC to go further?'

'To where, Sabine?' said Macleod. 'We checked the cottage. Rundown, derelict. The other one is owned by nobody in particular, some random bloke on an estate somewhere. It's a falsified record. They cover their tracks. I've checked with Anna Hunt, the head of our Service and she doesn't know.'

'What'd she tell you?' asked Sabine.

'This is somebody operating at a level up above the police who single-handedly killed off the McIntoshes. She would tell me if she knew. She would want to bring them down. People like Anna don't let those sorts of organisations flourish; they're unruly. The Service, whether or not you like it, thinks itself the correct people to arbitrate, because the Service at the end of the day, has some oversight. Someone pulls it to order.'

'It's not over though,' said Emmett.

'What makes you say that?' asked Macleod. 'What can we chase?'

'The letter,' said Emmett.

'We don't know where it came from. We have got no prints on it. A handwriting analysis, it could be anybody. We're dead in the water, as regards the investigation.'

'Maybe,' said Emmett, 'but I didn't say we would be the ones advancing it. Somebody sent you that letter. Somebody pushed you to investigate. They wanted a wrong put right.'

'And it's been put right.'

'I could live with that, and I could see it, if this was the one incident. This organisation, these people who did this, are still at large. They drove in a limousine with a hitman. They hired people. This is not something in the past that was trying to be protected. This is very much alive today,' said Emmett. 'And that scares me.'

'In what way?' asked Sabine.

'Because they want justice, like we do. You wouldn't lie down, Seoras. You went in there, knowing that you could be called a bluff in that cottage. And why did you put your life on the line? You said it! Things need to be put right for all the decent people out there. Well, some people want to put things right not for the decent people, but for revenge, for what's going on. Somebody put us up to this. Somebody protected us during it, which is the frightening bit. So, they have connections too. They could trace and follow us.'

'They weren't there at the end, though,' said Sabine.

'Depends on if you read the report about the house, the one before it got adjusted,' said Macleod.

'Before it got adjusted?' said Sabine.

'The cottage we were in, when that gunman came after us, well, it had some marks on it. Chips on the wall. Forensics said it could have happened from bullets, but there weren't many. I think the gunman left because they were under attack. Not because they looked at Emmett here and thought they couldn't handle him.'

'So, we were being followed,' said Emmett.

'I think you were followed a lot,' said Macleod. 'But you also followed me. Completely against my order. I said I was going in alone. You were to wait.'

'It was a stupid decision,' said Emmett.

'Yes, it was,' said Macleod. 'Well done, Emmett. I'm going back up the road. I'll see you tomorrow at the station. Have an evening. Do whatever you two do. Board games? I don't have a clue what it is that you actually play, but yes, whatever it is, go and do it. And thank you.'

Macleod put his hand forward, and Emmett shook it, and he then shook Sabine's. Emmett watched him as the man walked off, fedora hat still on his head, back to his car.

Emmett turned back to the grave of Simon Matthews.

'Is that us?' asked Sabine.

'It's coming. Something bigger's coming,' said Emmett.

'Maybe,' said Sabine. 'But I can wait for another day. Come on.'

She reached over and took his hand, giving it a squeeze. He smiled back.

'It's a very light scar, just under the underside of your chin where the glass cut,' said Emmett.

'Does it affect my looks?' Sabine teased.

'You know I'm not one to judge other people on their looks,' said Emmett. 'It really doesn't matter.'

'But does it affect them?' asked Sabine.

'No,' said Emmett.

He turned and walked beside her back to the car. She got into the driver's seat, started the engine as Emmett climbed in the other side, and they drove off to the A9. As the car pulled out of Pitlochry, Sabine began to hum a little tune.

'What's that?' asked Emmett.

'It's just a song. It's an old one but there's a woman that sings it. She's in Inverness tonight.'

'Do you want to go?' asked Emmett.

'You don't need to. It's not your sort of music. It's very quiet. More classical in some ways.'

'You want to go?' asked Emmett.

'I guess I do,' said Sabine.

'Then let's go,' said Emmett. 'You're always following me to do what I want. Let's see what you like.'

Sabine smiled as the car sped further up the A9.

Emmett picked her up that evening from her temporary accommodation. She'd been in the hotel room for the last three weeks and as Emmett knocked on the door, Sabine was fixing her hair. She wore a blue T-shirt, plain with black jeans, boots underneath. Her hair she felt she'd brushed to death because it never quite looked right, did it? She opened the door to Emmett, who was standing in a T-shirt with some sort of dragon on it and blue jeans.

'How do I look?' asked Sabine.

Emmett stared. For a moment, he looked flummoxed. He went to say something and then he stopped and then he said, 'Great.'

She wondered if he was going to say something more, and his cheeks were going slightly red.

'I never said to you,' Sabine whispered, 'I never said thank you. You saved my life by jumping on that gunman. If he had got that gun, I'd be dead.'

'You don't need to thank me. You're my colleague.'

'Just a colleague? You'd have done it for anyone?'

'I would have done it for anyone,' said Emmett, suddenly. 'You're also my friend. So I did it because you were my friend as well.'

'Well, thank you,' she said. 'I'd buy you something, but I wouldn't know what.'

'You don't need to buy me anything,' said Emmett. 'You'll be there for me. We're tight. You and me. Buddies. Close buddies. Yeah? There for each other. Now come on. You'll be late for your concert.'

He turned away. Sabine grabbed his hand, spinning him

back round, stepped forward and kissed him on the lips. She held the kiss for a moment before stepping back.

'Thank you,' she said.

Emmett looked confused, not knowing what to do. He looked at her again. She stared back, and there was an awkward silence.

'Concert,' said Sabine. 'Let's go to the concert.'

Emmett nodded. As he stepped out into the hallway of the hotel, he watched Sabine walk in front of him. His mind raced. He'd wanted the cold cases. He'd wanted to be the inspector, and he'd wanted Sabine with him, working alongside her. But this—what had just happened was—it was difficult to process. Yes, that was it, he thought. I just need time to process.

Sabine turned, put her hand out, and pulled Emmett forward along the corridor. 'Quick,' she said, 'or we'll be late.'

And Emmett ran along behind her.

Read on to discover the Patrick Smythe series!

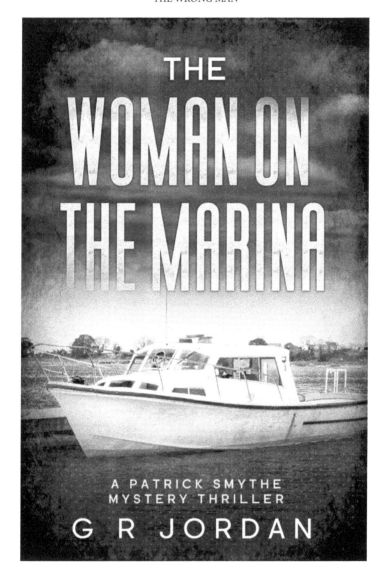

THE

WOMAN ON THE MARINA

A PATRICK SMYTHE
MYSTERY THRILLER

G R JORDAN

Patrick Smythe is a former Northern Irish policeman who after suffering an amputation after a bomb blast, takes to the sea between the west coast of Scotland and his homeland to ply his trade as a private investigator. Join Paddy as he tries to work to his own ethics while knowing how to bend the rules he once enforced. Working from his beloved motorboat 'Craigantlet', Paddy decides to rescue a drug mule in this short story from the pen of G R Jordan.

Join G R Jordan's monthly newsletter about forthcoming releases and special writings for his tribe of avid readers and then receive your free Patrick Smythe short story.

Go to https://bit.ly/PatrickSmythe for your Patrick Smythe journey to start!

About the Author

GR Jordan is a self-published author who finally decided at forty that in order to have an enjoyable lifestyle, his creative beast within would have to be unleashed. His books mirror that conflict in life where acts of decency contend with self-promotion, goodness stares in horror at evil, and kindness blindsides us when we at our worst. Corrupting our world with his parade of wondrous and horrific characters, he highlights everyday tensions with fresh eyes whilst taking his methodical, intelligent mainstays on a roller-coaster ride of dilemmas, all the while suffering the banter of their provocative sidekicks.

A graduate of Loughborough University where he masqueraded as a chemical engineer but ultimately played American football, Gary had worked at changing the shape of cereal flakes and pulled a pallet truck for a living. Watching vegetables freeze at -40'C was another career highlight and he was also one of the Scottish Highlands "blind" air traffic controllers.

These days he has graduated to answering a telephone to people in trouble before telephoning other people to sort it out.

Having flirted with most places in the UK, he is now based in the Isle of Lewis in Scotland where his free time is spent between raising a young family with his wife, writing, figuring out how to work a loom and caring for a small flock of chickens. Luckily, his writing is influenced by his varied work and life experience as the chickens have not been the poetical inspiration he had hoped for!

You can connect with me on:

🌐 https://grjordan.com

f https://facebook.com/carpetlessleprechaun

Subscribe to my newsletter:

✉ https://bit.ly/PatrickSmythe

Also by G R Jordan

G R Jordan writes across multiple genres including crime, dark and action adventure fantasy, feel good fantasy, mystery thriller and horror fantasy. Below is a selection of his work. Whilst all books are available across online stores, signed copies are available at his personal shop.

 **Drop Like Flies (Highlands & Islands Detective Book 42)**
https://grjordan.com/shop/highlands-islands-detective/drop-like-flies
A book to read left at a brutal death on the island of Barra. A follow up killing delivers the second volume for perusal. Can DI Hope McGrath catch the murderer before the series is completed?

Despite suffering from severe morning sickness, Mum-to-be DI Hope McGrath must embark on a far-reaching pursuit of a killer, tracing a path laid out in the books of a celebrated Scottish author. With a rising body count and the murderer closer than expected, can Hope decipher the clues hidden in the stories before someone she loves becomes the next victim?

Those who read beyond the words, see the real depth in a story!

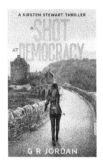

Kirsten Stewart Thrillers
https://grjordan.com/product/a-shot-at-democracy
Join Kirsten Stewart on a shadowy ride through the underbelly of the Highlands of Scotland where among the beauty and splendour of the majestic landscape lies corruption and intrigue to match any city. From murders to extortion, missing children to criminals operating above the law, the Highland former detective must learn a tougher edge to her work as she puts her own life on the line to protect those who cannot defend themselves.

Having left her beloved murder investigation team far behind, Kirsten has to battle personal tragedy and loss while adapting to a whole new way of executing her duties where your mistakes are your own. As Kirsten comes to terms with working with the new team, she often operates as the groups solo field agent, placing herself in danger and trouble to rescue those caught on the dark side of life. With action packed scenes and tense scenarios of murder and greed, the Kirsten Stewart thrillers will have you turning page after page to see your favourite Scottish lass home!

There's life after Macleod, but a whole new world of death!

Jac's Revenge (A Jac Moonshine Thriller #1)

https://grjordan.com/product/jacs-revenge

An unexpected hit makes Debbie a widow. The attention of her man's killer spawns a brutal yet classy alter ego. But how far can you play the game before it takes over your life?

All her life, Debbie Parlor lived in her man's shadow, knowing his work was never truly honest. She turned her head from news stories and rumours. But when he was disposed of for his smile to placate a rival crime lord, Jac Moonshine was born. And when Debbie is paid compensation for her loss like her car was written off, Jac decides that enough is enough.

Get on board with this tongue-in-cheek revenge thriller that will make you question how far you would go to avenge a loved one, and how much you would enjoy it!

 **A Giant Killing (Siobhan Duffy Mysteries #1)**
https://grjordan.com/product/a-giant-killing
A body lies on the Giant's boot. Discord, as the master of secrets has been found. Can former spy Siobhan Duffy find the killer before they execute her former colleagues?

When retired operative Siobhan Duffy sees the killing of her former master in the paper, her unease sends her down a path of discovery and fear. Aided by her young housekeeper and scruff of a gardener, Siobhan begins a quest to discover the reason for her spy boss' death and unravels a can of worms today's masters would rather keep closed. But in a world of secrets, the difference between revenge and simple, if brutal, housekeeping becomes the hardest truth to know.

The past is a child who never leaves home!